Bat Rider

Matthew John wishes to be a bat rider.
If he finds the cave where the bats live,
will his dream come true?
Or will he meet Oomba the lion?

ANTHONY BARTON

Bat Rider

WITH DECORATIONS BY THE AUTHOR

Bulmer Press

BAT RIDER

Bulmer Press Edition
Copyright © 2011 Anthony Barton
Library and Archives Canada Cataloguing in Publication
Barton, Anthony, 1942-
Bat rider / Anthony Barton; with decorations by the author.
ISBN 978-0-9869038-3-0
I. Title.
PS8553.A7776B38 2011   jC813'.6   C2011-903933-8
Cover and drawings by Anthony Barton. All Rights Reserved.

TO FREDESWINDA

Matthew John, the bats
and I made this book
for you
with love

Contents

CHAPTER I

Telling the Bats a Story

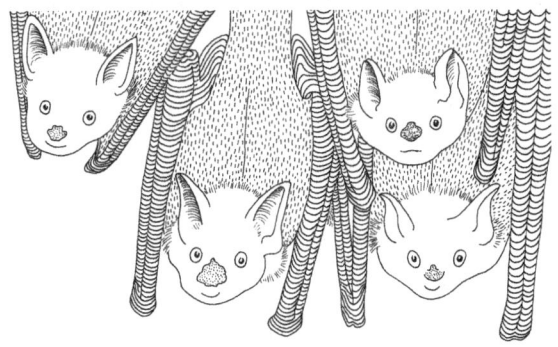

THE BATS flap their wings, jump up and down, and say 'Eep! Eep!'

'I promise I won't leave any of you out,' I tell them. Bats like listening to stories about themselves.

The gloomiest of the bats, Vesper, says that she thinks Matthew John will be eaten by the lion.

'Not at all,' I reply quickly. 'I am sure the lion won't do Matthew John or Bulmer any harm.'

'I wouldn't know about that,' says Vesper, narrowing her eyes. 'You never can tell with lions.'

The brightest of the bats, Hula, says that Matthew John should make friends with the lion.

'Sometimes it is not easy to make friends,' I point out. 'That's how Matthew John's first adventure began.'

'How?' chorus the bats. 'Tell us.'

'Before I begin, I think you should know that Matthew John is frightened of dark places. One day, when he was a baby, the lights went out and he thought there was a strange creature in his bedroom. He thought he could hear the creature creeping closer. He was too frightened to cry. Have any of you ever been too frightened to cry?'

Vesper and Hula look at me solemnly, their eyes as round as saucers.

'If you have,' I go on, 'then I expect you know how Matthew John feels about being in the dark. Even now, years later, he has only to think about the dark, and that is enough to make him gnaw his knuckles. Do you want to hear how he met Bulmer for the first time?'

The bats nod.

BAT RIDER

CHAPTER II

How Matthew John Met Bulmer

M ATTHEW JOHN was finishing his breakfast when his mother said 'Go out and play with the other boys and girls.'

'They won't play with me,' said Matthew John, with his mouth full. 'I am too small.'

'No you're not,' said his Mummy. 'Out you go, Matthew John!'

Matthew John swallowed his last mouthful and ran out of his home.

Another boy his own age saw him.

'You can't play with us,' said Joshua Ryan.

'Why not?' said Matthew John.

'You're too small,' said Joshua Ryan.

'I am not small,' said Matthew John.

'You are,' said Joshua Ryan. 'You're the smallest boy I've ever seen.'

'I am not,' said Matthew John. 'I'm going to be a bat rider.'

'You?' said Joshua Ryan. 'A bat rider? No bat would choose you.'

Joshua Ryan's sister Emily Charlotte clung to Joshua Ryan's back, pretending to be a bat rider. 'Turn left!' she said to her brother. The other boys and girls began to play Bat Rider, too. Matthew John watched them. He heard them shout 'Eep! Eep!' as they ran down the street and round a corner. Matthew John was left all alone. He felt sad. He wanted to play. 'I wish I wasn't so small,' he said to himself. He scratched an itchy place on his ankle.

He went to the Look Out Place and looked up. His heart leaped.   He could see the giant bats up in the sky.

The giant bats were flapping their great big wings. The bats were heading for the cave. Matthew John had never been to the cave. Matthew John knew that the bats and their riders had been out all night, gathering fruit. Every bat had a boy or girl riding on his or her back. Matthew John wished he could be up there with them, riding on the back of his own bat. He wanted so much to be a bat rider, but only a few, lucky children were chosen by the bats to ride on their backs and help harvest the Yumi fruit. He sighed.

Matthew John walked back to his house. 'Daddy, what should I do? Nobody will play with me. I'm too small.'

Daddy said dreamily 'Think tall and you won't feel small.'

'Oh, Daddy, you're so silly,' said Matthew John. 'Mum, what should I do? I want to be a bat rider.'

'Go and ask Mr. Seeds,' said Mummy. 'He's the wisest man in the village. I'll give you loaf of freshly baked bread for him. Put on your backpack. You can carry the loaf in that.'

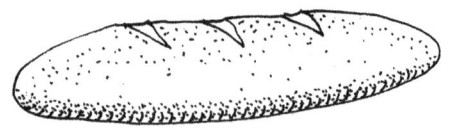

Matthew John fetched his backpack from his room. He put his arms through the straps and settled the pack on his back.

His mother put the loaf inside the pack. 'You know where to find Mr. Seeds?' she said.

'The house in the Sleepy Field?'

'That's where he lives. See you later.'

'See you later,' said Matthew John, and ran out of the house, the pack with the loaf inside bumping on his back.

The Sleepy Field was filled with flowers that made Matthew John feel sleepy. Matthew John tiptoed through the field. He held his nose. 'Bodder dese stupid flaurs,' he said. 'I dink I'm going to sneeze.'

He sneezed. 'Achoo!' He sneezed again. 'Achoo! Achoo!' He knocked on the door of Mr. Seeds's house.

'Who's that?' said a voice.

'It's me, Matthew John,' he said. 'Hurry up and

open the door. These flowers are making me sneeze.'

The door opened.

'The flowers are supposed to make you sleep,' said Mr. Seeds.

'They make me sneeze,' said Matthew John, and sneezed again. 'Achoo!'

Mr. Seeds smiled. 'You had better come in,' he said.

Matthew John wriggled out of the straps of his backpack, pulled out the loaf and gave it to Mr. Seeds. 'This is from my mother,' he said.

'I'll make us some sandwiches,' said Mr. Seeds. He wheeled his wheelchair to the kitchen and made sandwiches for them both. He made Matthew John a milkshake. They sat face to face in Mr. Seeds's kitchen. Matthew John sat on a kitchen stool. Mr. Seeds sat in his wheelchair.

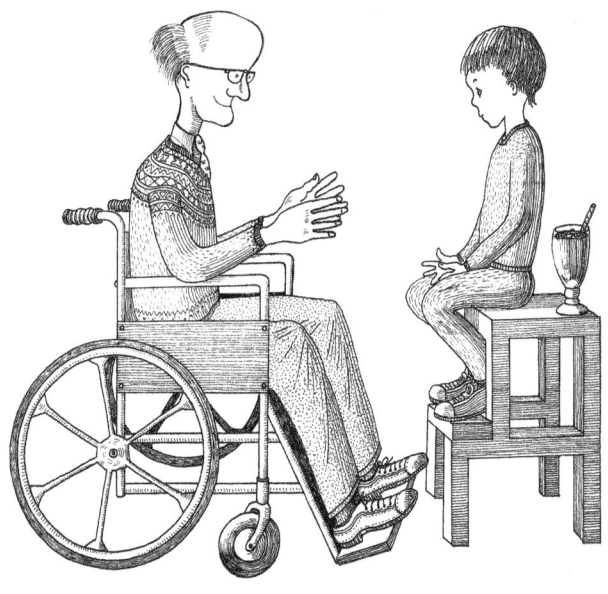

They ate their sandwiches. The sandwiches tasted of boiled egg and mayonnaise.

'What's the matter, Matthew John?' said Mr. Seeds.

'I want to be a bat rider,' said Matthew John.

He sucked at his milkshake through a straw. It was a peach milkshake, his favorite.

'You want to be a bat rider,' said Mr. Seeds, 'but the other boys and girls say you are too small?'

Matthew John nodded, wondering how Mr. Seeds knew so much. He bit his lip.

Mr. Seeds cocked his head to one side and looked at Matthew John. 'What are you frightened of, Matthew John?'

'I'm not frightened.'

'Everybody is frightened of something,' said Mr. Seeds gently.

Matthew John looked down at his milkshake, admiring the bubbly froth. There was something that frightened him. He was frightened of the dark. But he did not want to tell Mr. Seeds about that. 'How can I be a bat rider?' he said in a small voice. 'Can you help me?'

'A bat rider must be brave, kind and helpful,' said Mr. Seeds. 'Are you brave?'

'I don't know.'

'Are you kind?'

'Sometimes. I think.'

'Are you helpful?'

'I help Mummy wash the dishes.'

'When you have finished your milkshake,' said Mr. Seeds. 'I'll tell you what you have to do to be a bat rider.'

Matthew John sucked up the last of the milkshake, and gazed hopefully at Mr. Seeds. Would Mr. Seeds make his dream come true? Would Mr. Seeds help him become a bat rider? Matthew John hoped so. Matthew John stared into Mr. Seeds's eyes and waited.

'Follow Oomba's paw prints to the cave,' said Mr. Seeds.

'Who is Oomba?' said Matthew John.

'Oomba,' said Mr. Seeds, 'is a lion. He is very big lion. You do not want to meet Oomba.'

'Does Oomba make a sound?'

'He goes "Oomba! Oomba!" His footprints have six toes.' Mr. Seeds wheeled his chair into a back room and came back with a jar of ointment.

'This is Make-You-Better butter,' he said. 'Put your backpack on again and I'll put the jar inside your pack. I made the Make-You-Better butter myself. It is a good ointment for treating sprains and wounds.'

'Thank you, Mr. Seeds,' said Matthew John, wriggling into the straps and settling his pack on his back once more. He felt Mr. Seeds put the jar of ointment inside the pack. He felt the weight of the jar pull the straps tight about his shoulders.

'When you reach the cave, go inside,' said Mr. Seeds.

'Is it dark inside the cave?' said Matthew John, straightening his back and lifting his chin.

'Yes,' said Mr. Seeds. He looked concerned. 'Is that what you fear, Matthew John? The dark?'

'Yes,' mumbled Matthew John.

'Don't worry,' said the Mr. Seeds. 'Lots of people fear the dark.' Mr. Seeds pressed his fingertips to his forehead. 'Do you know that bats can see in the dark by listening?'

'By listening?' said Matthew John, surprised.

'That's why bats go "Eep! Eep!"' said Mr. Seeds. 'They listen for the echoes of their cries. One kind of echo means a tree. Another kind of echo means a fruit. The bat can tell which.'

'Bats must be clever if they can see with their ears,' said Matthew John.

'They are so clever,' said Mr. Seeds, 'that they can talk to their riders.'

'They can?'

'Yes,' said Mr. Seeds. 'Are you ready to begin your adventure?'

'Just a minute,' said Matthew John. He carried his empty milkshake glass to the sink. He rinsed the glass clean. His Mummy had taught him to be tidy.

'Thank you,' said Mr. Seeds. 'Are you ready now?'

Matthew John dried his hands on a towel and nodded. 'I'm ready,' he said.

'You had better leave this way,' said Mr. Seeds, wheeling his chair to the back door of his house.

'I see the paw prints of Oomba,' said Matthew John, stepping out into Mr. Seeds's back garden and pointing at the cat prints in the damp ground. 'His prints are awfully big.'

'Follow his paw prints to the cave,' said Mr. Seeds. 'Good luck, Matthew John.'

'Thank you, Mr. Seeds,' said Matthew John.

The trail of the six-toed paw prints led him out through the gate at the bottom of Mr. Seeds's garden and in among the Yumi trees. Matthew John was excited. His adventure had begun. He would be brave. He would be kind. He would show Joshua Ryan and Emily Charlotte that being small did not mean you could not be a bat rider. He broke into a run. He felt his pack with the jar of Make-You-Better butter inside it bump against his back as he raced for the cave.

Matthew John paused at the mouth of the cave to catch his breath. He had never visited the cave.

It looked dark in there. He was not sure he wanted to go in. Maybe being a bat rider was not such a good idea. Maybe he should run back to Mr. Seeds and tell him he had changed his mind. 'I'll just go a little way inside,' he told himself. He stepped into the darkness. The cave was beautiful. He looked up. His jaw dropped. Glowworms shone overhead like stars in the sky. Fireflies drifted through the darkness, winking on and off. Slender spires of rock rose from the floor, glittering with shiny crystals. Fluted curtains of green, blue and pink stone decorated the walls. Water fell tinkling into a pool. Blindfishes darted in the pool. The blindfish had no eyes. Fishes that live in caves do not need eyes. Matthew John watched one blindfish leap into the air with a flash of silvery scales, and then splash back into the water.

The splash echoed in the darkness.

Matthew John was entranced. What a lovely place this cave is, he thought. But where are the bats, and where are the boys and girls who ride on the backs of the bats?

Matthew John followed an underground river deep into the mountain. The daylight from the cave entrance faded behind him. The darkness thickened. He felt his way cautiously forward and found himself entering a great hall with walls and floor covered in moss that glowed pale blue. The moss felt springy under his gym shoes. He left dark footprints behind him in the moss as he crossed the hall. He noticed other, bigger footprints in the moss, footprints with six toes. He heard a sound of breathing. The hairs on the back of his neck rose. His legs felt wobbly. Where was that sound coming from? Who was breathing? He raised his eyes. By the light of the glowing moss he saw the bat riders. Dozens of boys and girls were fast asleep. They slept in rows of hanging beds that were slung from the ceiling.

The beds were accessed from hanging walkways. Both the beds and the walkways were woven from the tough bark of the Yumi tree. One boy snored and rolled over in his sleep. His hanging bed swayed, and sent the other beds swinging. So that is how a bat rider sleeps through the day, Matthew John thought, after a long night riding on his bat's back and harvesting fruit.

Matthew John was envious. He wished he were up there sleeping in his own hanging bed, with his own bat on call. Speaking of which, where were the riders' bats?

Matthew John walked under an arch of stone into another chamber. The moss in this chamber was a glimmering lemon yellow, and by its light Matthew John saw the bats.

Wow, he thought. They sleep upside down.

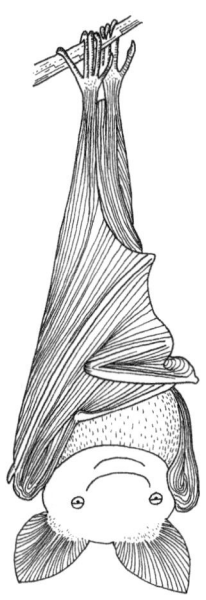

The bats hung from nooks and crannies in the ceiling, their feet locked in position to hold them safely dangling while they slept. They were big.

Each bat had folded its wings about its body, which was sensible, for it was chilly in the cave, even in the heat of the day.

Matthew John heard a faint sound somewhere in the cave and stood still, his heart racing. Some creature was moving in the darkness. Matthew John could hear the creature coming closer. He looked over his shoulder. He saw two eyes shining in the dark.

'Who are you?' said Matthew John.

'I'm Bulmer. Number Five Squadron. What's your outfit?'

'My outfit?' said Matthew John, puzzled.

'Who do you fly with?' said Bulmer. 'Wait a minute. What's happened to your wings?'

'I don't have wings,' said Matthew John.

'No wings?' said Bulmer, shocked. 'What kind of a bat has no wings?'

'I'm not a bat.'

'You're not a bat? What are you?'

'I'm a boy.'

'A boy?' Bulmer hopped closer to have a look. 'So you are. A boy. You must be a bat rider?'

'Not yet,' said Matthew John. 'But I do want to be a bat rider. I've always wanted to be a rider,' he added hopefully, watching Bulmer stretch his huge velvety, bony wings. He saw Bulmer wince. 'What's the matter?'

'My left wing hurts,' said Bulmer.

Matthew John wriggled out of the straps of his pack and unscrewed the lid from the jar of Make-You-

Better butter that Mr. Seeds had given him. 'I brought this medicine. I don't know if it will do any good.'

'Slather it on,' said Bulmer. 'My squadron needs me.'

Matthew John scooped a handful of the butter from the jar and began to rub it gently on Bulmer's sore wing.

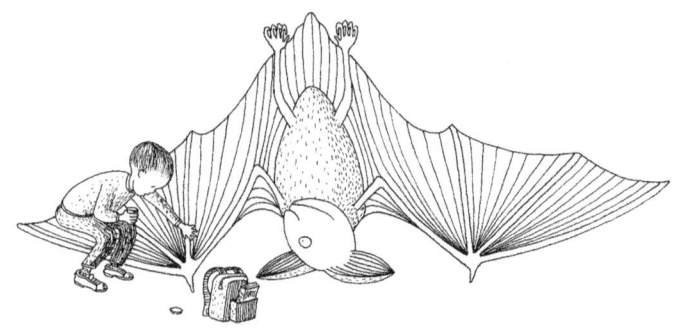

'My name's Matthew John. How did you hurt yourself, Bulmer?'

'I forgot to lock my feet,' said Bulmer. 'A little more to the right, please. Up a bit. There. That's where it hurts. Ow!' He sucked in his breath.

'Sorry,' said Matthew John. 'I'll try to be more gentle. This is my first time being a nurse. Did you say you forgot to lock your feet? How do you lock your feet?'

'I'm not sure,' Bulmer sighed. 'All the other bats know how to lock their feet. They dangle upside down from the roof of the cave, and lock their feet before they go to sleep.'

'This was my first night on my own,' Bulmer went on. 'I tried to lock my feet. I'm sure I heard my bones click. But I must have done something wrong, for as soon as I fell asleep, my feet relaxed and then down I came. Bump! I hit the cave floor hard and my wing is hurting. I'm going to be the laughing-stock of the squadron when they wake. They'll point at me. "Look at the bat who couldn't lock his feet!" they'll say. "Bulmer the drop-out!" That's what they'll call me.'

'We'll fix your wing before they wake, and they'll never know,' said Matthew John, digging the last of the Make-You-Better butter from the jar and rubbing it carefully into Bulmer's warm brown skin. 'There. How do you feel now?' He screwed the top back on, put the empty jar in his pack, and replaced the backpack on his shoulders.

Bulmer tried stretching his wing.

'Will you be able to fly?'

'I don't know,' said Bulmer.

'You don't know?'

'Well, I haven't actually done any flying,' said Bulmer. 'Not yet. To tell you the truth, Matthew John, the whole idea of swooping about in all that empty space gives me the creeps.'

'You're afraid to fly?' said Matthew John. 'But you're a bat.'

Bulmer swallowed. 'Yes.'

'Don't worry,' said Matthew John, trying to sound as reassuring as Mr. Seeds. 'Lots of people fear to fly. Oh dear, I dink I'm gowin da thneeze.'

Matthew John took a handkerchief from his pocket. 'Excuthe me. Muth be that Make-You-Bether buther. It may be making you bether, but it's making me – '

Matthew John blew his nose loudly. The sound of his sneeze echoed through the cave.

Bulmer grasped Matthew John's arm with the claw of the thumb of his right wing. 'I think something is coming.'

Matthew John froze, listening. From somewhere in the deep dark depths of the cave a beast gave voice.

'Oomba! Oomba!' said the beast.

Oomba the cave lion was dozing off when he heard the sneeze. Lions like to hunt in the cool of the morning and sleep during the day. He had enjoyed a light meal. For an appetizer he had eaten four zebras and nice crunchy gazelle. His main course had been a white rhinoceros weighing two and a half tons, aged in the sun and sprinkled with mongongo nuts. For dessert he had swallowed a dozen guinea fowl. After his meal he had returned to his cave by way of the forest of Yumi trees, leaving a trail of six-toed paw prints behind him. He had gone to the very back of his cave where it was cool and dark. This was his favorite spot to curl up and have a little nap. He had smiled to himself and stretched his weary limbs out on the moss. He had yawned. The annoying bats and children that hung about the roof of his cave had all been asleep. The gentle tinkle of water falling into the pool had soothed him. He had just started dreaming of about how nice it would be to meet a lioness one day and start a family, when he had heard a loud 'Achoo!' and had woken feeling angry and upset.

Who has dared enter my cave? thought Oomba. He was a cave lion, and he took his cave seriously. It was *his* cave and nobody was allowed to come into *his* cave without *his* permission. He opened his mouth and spoke his own name aloud so that the intruder would know whose cave he had entered. 'Oomba!' he roared. 'Oomba!'

Oomba stood up. He lashed his tail. He breathed in through his nose, testing the air. He could smell the stranger who had entered his cave. The stranger smelled of boiled eggs, mayonnaise, and peach milkshake. Oomba growled. What a nerve! Peach milkshake, in *his* cave. Oomba began to walk softly through the darkness on his huge padded feet, digging his claws into the glowing moss with every step he took.

His ears strained. He could hear someone else with the stranger, someone who had wings and claws that scraped across his cave floor. One of those tiresome bats, I expect, Oomba thought. One of those bats that go 'Eep! Eep!' and fly out of my cave in the evening, and return to my cave at dawn.

He leaped across the underground river in a single bound, dashed through the Flowstone Hall, and spotted the intruder, a mere boy, wearing some kind of pack on his back. The boy was helping a bat climb the Crystal Stair.

I have you now, Peach Milkshake, thought Oomba, and broke into a run, his claws extended.

Matthew John was helping Bulmer up the Crystal Stair. Bats can walk, but it is a struggle. Their legs are hobbled by their wings. The best a bat can do when on the ground is stumble. 'Nearly there,' Matthew John said. He heaved Bulmer onto the top step.

An angry roar shook the cave. Delicate rock formations trembled and crystal shards tinkled to the floor. Matthew John turned. Oomba the lion was racing towards them.

'Watch out for Oomba,' Mr. Seeds had said, and here was Oomba dashing at them, and looking very big and dangerous.

'We're done for,' said Matthew John.

'Not at all,' said Bulmer. 'Hop on my back. I'll fly us out.'

'You have never flown before,' said Matthew John. 'You said so.'

'How hard can it be?' said Bulmer. 'I'll be a flying ace. You'll see.'

Matthew John jumped onto Bulmer's back. 'Go, Bulmer!' he said, putting his arms around the giant bat's neck.

'Chocks away!' said Bulmer, and flopped over the edge of the Crystal Tower. He spread his wings wide.

Oomba lunged, reaching out to grab Bulmer and Matthew John with his forepaws, but he lost his footing and fell into the ravine.

With a splash Oomba hit the river. Moments later he surfaced and blew water from his nose.

Bulmer zoomed over Oomba's head. 'Tat! Tat! Tat!' he said, skimming past the lion's ears. 'Take that, you big cat!'

Head above water, paws paddling, and his tail sticking straight out behind, Oomba gave a roar of defiance as he was swept away around a bend in the river.

'Wahoo! Wait until my squadron hears about this,' said Bulmer, and he waggled his wings in a victory roll.

'Bulmer, what are you doing?' said Matthew John, hanging on tightly. The river was above his head and the sky beneath his feet. 'I'm upside-down.'

'I'm looping the loop,' said Bulmer. 'I told you I was a flying ace.'

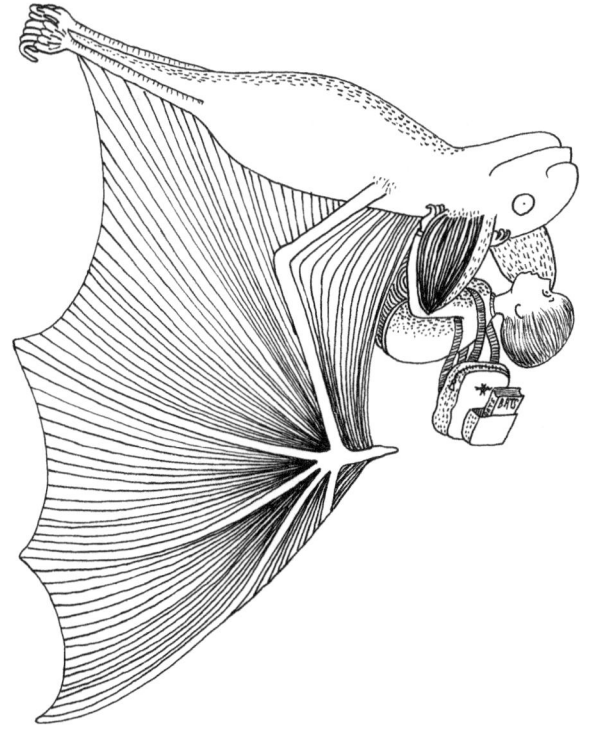

'I must not let go,' Matthew John said to himself. 'I must hang on tight. I'm a bat rider. I must keep a tight grip on my bat.'

Matthew John and Bulmer flew out of the cave.

Bulmer swooped headlong into the shade of the forest. The towering trunks of the massive mile-high Yumi trees whipped past to right and left. 'Eep! Eep!' cried Bulmer, and rocketed skyward, leaving the trees and soaring up into a bright blue sky.

When they leveled off at ten thousand feet, Matthew John was glad to find himself the right way up. He looked about him and felt wonderful. He was high in the air, seated astride the neck of a giant bat. He could feel the warmth of the sun on his arms. Fresh air rushed past his face. This was what it was like to be a bat rider. It was awesome. He was flying.

'Let's do a swoop!' said Bulmer.
'Okay,' said Matthew John.

They did a swoop, swishing past the leaves of a Yumi tree and then skyrocketing up again.

'Let's fly through a cloud,' said Matthew John.

They flew through the cloud. It was white, damp and foggy inside. They could not see where they were going. They burst out of the cloud into the sunshine.

'Look at me!' said Bulmer. The bat was excited. This was his first flight. The other bats would be proud of him. 'I am shutting my eyes. I'm using my ears to see where I'm going. Eep! Eep! I hear an echo ahead.'

'Watch out,' said Matthew John. 'You're going to hit a tree.'

'Me? The pride of Fifth Squadron?' said Bulmer. 'Hit a tree?'

There was a thump. Matthew John lost his grip.

Matthew John flew through the air and landed on his back among Yumi flowers. Each Yumi flower had five blue petals. 'Bulmer!' he called. 'Where are you?' he said. He jumped to his feet. 'Bulmer?'

There was no answer.

Matthew John was a bat rider without a bat. He looked about him anxiously. He saw a dewpond with a family of swans honking and pulling at something with their beaks. They were making sounds like a squeaky gate. He saw flowerbeds bright with morning glories and decorated with maidenhair ferns. I'm in some kind of a garden, he thought. He looked up and saw branches bending under the weight of ripe, purple Yumi fruit. Each Yumi fruit had five fat fingers. The Yumi fruit made Matthew John's mouth water. Mmm! They looked good. Mr. Seeds had told him that the Yumi trees bore flowers and fruit at the same time. What a pity the fruit were out of reach. As he stared up at the fruit, he noticed that the sky was moving.

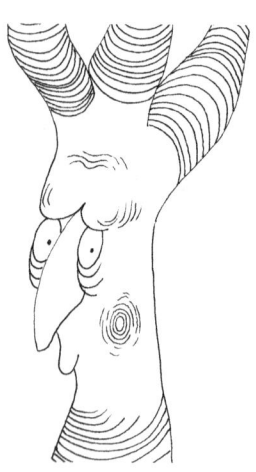

'What is this place?' he said.

'This is a tree garden,' said a voice.

Matthew John turned and saw that the Yumi tree had a face. 'You have lost your friend,' said the tree.

'Yes, I have,' said Matthew John. 'He's a bat. His name is Bulmer.'

'What is your name?' said the Yumi tree.

'Matthew John.'

'My name is Boris,' said the Yumi tree. 'At the top of every tree in this forest there is a garden. This is mine. I hope you like my swans. They flew in one day and made themselves at home. I think your friend

Bulmer just splashed down in their dewpond. They are pulling him to the shore.'

Matthew John ran to the edge of the pond. 'Bulmer!' he said. 'Are you all right?'

'Bit of a prang,' said Bulmer, thickly. 'The swans say I should have slowed my wing beats and twisted my wings to catch more wind. That would have slowed me down. I'll have to try that next time.' Bulmer flopped out of the pond and fell on his nose.

'Take my hand,' said Matthew John, and hauled his friend back up onto his feet.

Bulmer shook himself and drops of water flew in all directions.

'I hope you did not hurt yourself landing, Bulmer,' said the tree.

'Not at all,' said Bulmer. 'Who are you?' he asked, staring about him.

'I'm the tree you landed on. Boris is my name.'

'I hope I didn't hurt you, Boris.'

'Not in the slightest. Have you and your rider come for some of my Yumi fruit?'

Matthew John and Bulmer exchanged glances.

'May we have some?' asked Matthew John.

'You may have some of my fruit,' said Boris, 'but only if you promise to save and plant the seeds. The seeds inside the fruit are my way of making more trees like me.'

'We shall save the seeds,' said Bulmer. 'Squadron's honor.'

'And plant them, too,' said Matthew John. 'I promise.'

'Good,' said Boris, and three ripe Yumi fruit fell from a branch and landed at their feet. 'Put the three fruit in your backpack, Matthew John. You will need your hands free to hold onto Bulmer while you are flying.'

Matthew John did as he was told, and then he and Bulmer crawled to the edge of Boris's tree garden and looked down at Bat Mountain, the winding river and the village far below.

'Everything looks so small from up here,' said Matthew John. He could smell the three ripe Yumi fruit in his pack. 'Shall I climb on your back?'

'Yes,' said Bulmer. 'When you are ready, I'll flop over the edge.'

'I'm ready,' said Matthew John, his arms tightly wrapped around Bulmer's wet, furry neck. He was not going to lose his hold on his friend this time.

'Here we go,' said the bat.

'This is a present,' said Matthew John.

'A fresh Yumi fruit?' said Mr. Seeds, his face filled with delight. 'For me?' He wheeled his chair out onto the patio and into the sunshine. He turned the star-shaped fruit over in his hands and admired its purple color and its delicate powdery surface.

'Boris says you must save the seeds and plant them,' said Matthew John.

'I shall save the seeds,' said Mr. Seeds, 'and I shall plant them. But who is Boris?'

'Boris is the tree the fruit came from.'

'Do you mean to say that the tree talked to you? How lucky you are!'

'This is my bat, Bulmer.'

'I'm very pleased to meet you, Bulmer,' said Mr. Seeds. 'Are you two are a team?'

Bulmer grinned. 'We'll be flying with Number Five Squadron tonight. Your Make-You-Better butter cured me. Thanks.'

Mr. Seeds's jaw dropped. 'Matthew John. Do you mean to tell me that you are a – '

Matthew John put his arm round Bulmer's shoulder. 'Yes, I'm a bat rider,' he said proudly, 'and I am riding the best bat in the world.'

'Congratulations to you both,' said Mr. Seeds. 'Do you have time for a milkshake? Some cress and walnut sandwiches?'

'Thank you, Mr. Seeds, but it is getting late. Here's your empty jar back. We had better be on our way to tell my parents.' Matthew John gave Mr. Seeds a big hug. 'We could not have done it without you,' he whispered in Mr. Seeds's ear. 'Thanks for the warning about the lion Oomba.'

'I hope you didn't meet him?' Mr. Seeds looked aghast.

'We'll tell you about that another time,' said Matthew John, leaping onto his bat's back. 'Scramble, Bulmer!'

The bat leaped from the patio, and, with powerful beats of his wings, shot into the sky.

Matthew John's Mummy and Daddy were amazed by the arrival of their son riding on a bat.

'I brought you a Yumi fruit,' said Matthew John. 'It's fresh. You must save the seeds and bury them in the ground so they can sprout into baby Yumi trees.'

'I'll plant the seeds,' said Mummy, and put the Yumi fruit carefully in the fruit bowl on the dining room table. 'Matthew John,' she said, gazing at him as if he were a stranger. 'How did you become a bat rider?'

'I met Bulmer. You can shake claws with him. Bulmer, this is my mother.'

'Is it really safe for you, Bulmer?' Mummy asked. 'Flying up to the top of those tall trees? Aren't you scared?'

'Only when I fall on my nose,' said Bulmer. 'I'm not good at landings.' He blushed.

'All the best, Bulmer,' said Daddy, shaking Bulmer's claw.

'See you,' said Matthew John, leaping astride Bulmer's neck.

'Take us away, Bulmer!'

'Come back soon!' shouted Mummy, waving.

'We'll be waiting!' shouted Daddy.

Matthew John saw Joshua Ryan and Emily Charlotte playing Bat Rider in the street.

'Touch down!' said Bulmer, making his best landing yet, right in front of Joshua Ryan.

Joshua Ryan was amazed. 'Matthew John?' he said. 'You're a - bat rider?'

Emily Charlotte slid down from her brother's back and ran to pet Bulmer. 'The fur feels so soft,' she said, stroking Bulmer's head.

'Thanks,' said Bulmer, and Emily Charlotte's eyes widened. A bat had spoken to her.

Matthew John pulled the third and last Yumi fruit from his backpack. 'This is for you two. Save the seeds and plant them in the soil.'

'I want to be a bat rider,' said Joshua Ryan.

'So do I,' said Emily Charlotte.

Matthew John grinned. 'Go and see Mr. Seeds. He'll tell you what to do. Sorry we can't stay to play.'

'Got to join the Squadron,' said Bulmer.

The pair soared aloft and rose high above the Yumi trees.

CHAPTER III

The Rescue of Annabelle Sue

BULMER swooped down toward the place where the bats lived. 'Don't worry, kid,' he said. 'I can do this. Piece of cake.'

'Who's worried?' said Matthew John, and wrapped his arms more tightly around Bulmer's neck, hoping for the best. Bulmer was the best bat in the whole world. Bulmer could swoop through the air. Bulmer could fly upside down. Bulmer could loop the loop. But Bulmer was not so hot when it came to landings. They had already had one crash landing, in a pond. Matthew John did not want another.

They flew into the dark cave. Matthew John could not see well in the dark but Bulmer could. Bats can see with their ears better than they can see with their eyes.

'Eep! Eep!' said Bulmer, listening for the echoes of his cries bouncing back from the cave walls.

'Don't forget to lock your feet,' said Matthew John.

'Hang on!' said Bulmer.

Matthew John hung on.

Bulmer zoomed up towards the cave ceiling, his wings beating fast as he turned over in the air and stuck out his legs. He hooked the claws of his feet onto the edge of a ledge.

Matthew John found himself upside down. His tummy felt funny. He heard two bony clicks. Bulmer had remembered to lock his feet.

Bulmer relaxed, hanging by his feet. He folded his wings away like umbrellas. 'We've landed,' he said. 'You may let go of my neck now, Matthew John.'

Matthew John was not sure that he wanted to let go. It was dark. He couldn't see. He was hugging a bat that was hanging from the ceiling of a cave. It must be a long drop down to the rock floor below. 'I'll fall,' he said.

'You'll fall into your hammock,' said Bulmer. 'Trust me.'

Matthew John let go. He fell into his hammock. The hammock felt soft, and swung gently to and fro. This is what it is like being a bat rider, thought

Matthew John. I am swinging in my hammock. I have joined Number Five Squadron.

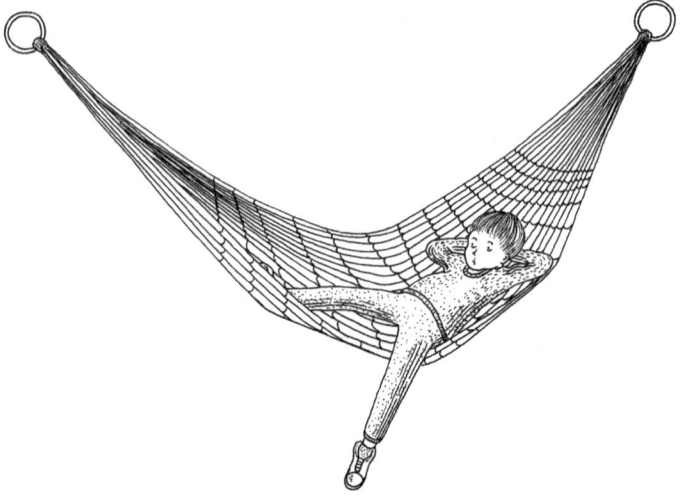

He frowned. 'Bulmer?'

'Uh-huh.'

'Who is in charge of the Squadron? Who is the boss?'

'The squadron leader is the boss.'

'I wish I were squadron leader.'

'Your fellow bat riders might think you too small to be squadron leader,' said Bulmer.

'Being small didn't stop me from becoming a bat rider. Why should it stop me from becoming a squadron leader? Bulmer, why don't grown-ups ride bats?'

'Grown-ups are too heavy. We can't lift them into the air. Our wings aren't strong enough.'

'I'm glad I'm a bat rider,' said Matthew John. 'My friends Joshua Ryan and Emily Charlotte want to be bat riders, too. I do hope their wish comes true.' He closed his eyes and dreamed of being squadron leader and leading a whole bunch of bats on an important mission to save the world.

'Bat Alert!' said a squeaky voice. 'All riders report to the Briefing Room.'

Matthew John woke from his dream with a start. 'All riders do what?' he said.

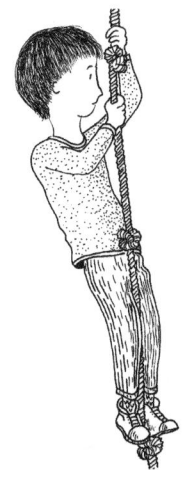

'They have sounded the Bat Alert. There's some kind of flap on,' said Bulmer. 'You have to go up into the loft with the other riders.'

Matthew John sat up in his hammock and looked about him. Lanterns had been lit. Boys and girls were climbing up knotted ropes that dangled through holes in the ceiling.

A red BAT ALERT lamp was flashing.

'You had better climb up your rope,' said Bulmer.

'I have my own rope?' said Matthew John. 'Good. But why don't we fly up there together?'

'It's a briefing for riders only,' said Bulmer. 'I just hang about down here until you come back and tell me what our mission is.'

'Right.' Matthew John climbed up the rope. He followed the other young people into the loft. The Briefing Room was a cavern shaped like a theatre. Matthew John took a seat on a curved bench among the audience. He saw his two friends coming.

'Matthew John!' said Joshua Ryan.

'We're bat riders, too,' said Emily Charlotte. 'We just joined the squadron.'

Matthew John was delighted to see them both. 'Sit here beside me,' he said. 'I'm so glad you are bat riders. How did you find your way to the cave?'

'We followed your footprints,' said Joshua Ryan. 'My bat's name is Smoky. He's waiting for me down below.'

'My bat's name is Vesper,' said Emily Charlotte. 'She's waiting for me, too.'

'Welcome to the squadron,' said Matthew John. 'I can't wait to meet your bats. I wonder what the fuss is about. That must be the squadron leader on the stage. Why is she so upset?'

Emily Charlotte lowered her voice. 'We brought her an urgent message from Chef Wandor.'

'Who is Chef Wandor?'

'He's famous for his Yumi pies. He runs a restaurant.'

'What was the message about?'

'It was about the chef's daughter. I think she's lost in the storm.'

'The storm?' said Matthew John, frowning. He had not heard anything about a storm. How long had he slept?

'The storm began an hour ago,' said Joshua Ryan, 'with thunder and lightning. We were pretty scared coming through the wood. All the Yumi trees were groaning and tossing their heads.'

'Ssh!' said Emily Charlotte. 'The squadron leader is about to speak.'

The squadron leader was a stout teenager with brown hair and green eyes. She folded her arms and waited for silence.

'I have grave news,' she said. 'Chef Wandor's

daughter Annabelle Sue is lost in the Back of Beyond. I need three volunteers to fly a special mission to find her.'

Matthew John exchanged glances with Joshua Ryan and Emily Charlotte. Annabelle Sue was their classmate at school. They rose to their feet.

'We volunteer!' they said.

'Thank you,' said the squadron leader. 'You may begin your search for Annabelle Sue as soon as the storm blows over.'

'We can't wait until then,' said Matthew John. 'Annabelle Sue may be in trouble. We must leave now and brave the storm. Will you come with us, squadron leader?'

'I can't,' said the squadron leader. 'I have grown so stout that I have become heavy for my bat Hula to bear. We would only slow you down.'

'Then we shall go by ourselves,' said Matthew John, and he turned to his friends. 'Joshua Ryan and Emily Charlotte, are you ready?'

'Ready,' said Joshua Ryan.

'Ready,' said Emily Charlotte.

'Let's go!' said Matthew John.

Matthew John, Joshua Ryan and Emily Charlotte ran for their ropes, shinnied down, leaped on the backs of their bats and took to the air.

'Follow me!' cried Matthew John.

The three bat riders flew out of the cave and into the storm.

The wind was strong and carried them along. They were blown through the air. They passed over the street where they lived.

Matthew John waved to his Mummy and Daddy. His parents waved back. His Mummy looked worried to see her son riding his bat in such fierce weather.

'I'll be all right,' he shouted. 'Take shelter inside the house. The wind is blowing things about.'

Joshua Ryan waved to his own parents, and Emily Charlotte waved to hers.

They were blown over the Sleepy Field, and saw Mr. Seeds out in his garden tying his plants to sticks so they would not be knocked down by the wind.

Mr. Seeds looked up at them. 'Watch out for the bees!' he shouted.

'Watch out for the what?' shouted Matthew John.

Mr. Seeds was a good friend who had helped him

become a bat rider. Mr. Seeds was also a wise man and Matthew John took his advice seriously.

'The bees!' hollered Mr. Seeds.

'Did he say cheese?' said Matthew John to himself, puzzled. 'Watch out for the cheese? I wonder why he said that. How can cheese be dangerous?'

The wind blew the three bat riders out over the ocean.

'We'll be drowned,' said Emily Charlotte's bat Vesper.

'Vesper says we'll be drowned,' said Emily Charlotte.

Matthew John put up a hand to keep the wind out of his eyes. Was that an island on the horizon? The gale was blowing them towards it. 'Joshua Ryan! Emily Charlotte!' he said. 'Head for the island.'

As they skimmed low over the island beach, Matthew John caught sight of an animal wading ashore. The animal was large and fierce with a mane of golden hair and a tail that stuck out straight behind. The animal looked familiar, but Matthew John had other things to think about. He spotted a sign that read JELLY BELLY RESTAURANT.

'What a name for a restaurant!' said Joshua Ryan's bat Smoky.

'Are we going to land?' asked Joshua Ryan.

'Yes,' said Matthew John.

'I'll try to hit something soft,' said Bulmer.

Matthew John and Bulmer hurtled into the restaurant and rushed toward a sponge cake decorated with whipped cream and raspberries.

'Hang on!' said Bulmer.

Matthew John and Bulmer crashed into the dessert. Sponge cake and raspberries exploded in all directions. Matthew John tried to speak, but his mouth was full of whipped cream. He pulled a raspberry from his hair and popped the raspberry in his mouth to join the cream. He swallowed. Mmm! The raspberry and the cream went well together. He scooped a handful of raspberries away from his bat's eyes. 'Are you okay, Bulmer?'

'I'm in heaven,' said Bulmer, licking cream from one of his wings with his purple tongue.

'Joshua Ryan and Smoky? Are you still in one piece?'

'We soft-landed in a lemon meringue pie,' said Joshua Ryan.

'It was a beautiful experience,' said Smoky.

'Emily Charlotte and Vesper?' said Matthew John.

'We're digging ourselves out of a chocolate mousse,' said Emily Charlotte.

'Here comes the chef,' said Vesper, gloomily. 'He looks upset. I expect we're in trouble.'

A grown-up with a big tummy wearing a tall white hat waddled towards them. He waved a long wooden spoon at them. 'Imbeciles!' he shouted. 'What is this that you do? You spoil my Raspberry Surprise. You make hole in my Vanilla Cream Pie. You squash my Chocolate Dream.'

'We didn't mean to,' said Matthew John. 'We are very sorry. It was the wind. We had to land in a hurry.'

'I am the great Wandor,' said the chef, beating his hand with his spoon, 'and this is a restaurant, not a playground. Kitchen duty for you three. I make you wash dishes. I put your bats in pantry. I grill your bats. I serve your bats with roasted walnuts.'

'Chef Wandor,' said Matthew John. 'You are not allowed to cook our bats. We are bat riders on a mission. We have come help you find your daughter. You sent a message to our squadron leader.'

Chef Wandor threw his spoon to the ground, and buried his face in his hands. His shoulders shook. 'Our only daughter, Annabelle Sue,' he said. 'She went to look for truffles and fell into Back of Beyond. Her mother will never forgive me.'

Matthew John patted the chef on the back. 'Don't worry. We'll find your Annabelle Sue for you. We'll bring her home safe and sound. You'll see.'

Chef Wandor spread his fingers and looked between them at Matthew John. 'You bring back my little girl?' he said.

Matthew John looked at Joshua Ryan and Emily Charlotte.

They nodded.

'Yes, we shall bring her home,' said Matthew John, looking the chef straight in the eye. 'Just tell us where to look. Where is this Back of Beyond?'

'Come,' said Chef Wandor. 'I show you.'

The chef picked up his spoon and led the three bat riders down a path that wound its way through his restaurant garden. A gust of wind nearly knocked them down. Bulmer, Smoky and Vesper humped along as best they could.

They opened an iron gate and stepped into a forest of groaning Yumi trees. The trees swayed from side to side, buffeted by the storm. Their roots heaved and strained. A flash of light lit the forest. The sky crashed and rumbled.

'Here is place where Annabelle Sue fell,' said Chef Wandor. He pointed with his spoon at a gap between the tree roots. 'I try to go after her, but I am too big. I can't squeeze through hole.'

'Where does the hole lead to?'

'Hole lead to Back of Beyond.' The chef looked as if he might burst into tears again at any moment.

'What is Annabelle Sue's favorite dessert?' said Emily Charlotte.

'Yumi Pie,' said the chef. 'She love my Yumi Pie.'

'Go and bake a Yumi Pie for her,' said Emily Charlotte, 'while we fetch her home to eat it.'

Chef Wandor's face lit up. 'You find my girl. I bake pie.' He hurried off, heading back towards the Jelly Belly Restaurant.

'I hope we can find his daughter,' said Joshua Ryan.

'We have to,' said Emily Charlotte.

'We shall,' said Matthew John, jumping on Bulmer's back. 'Down the hole, Bulmer! And remember what Mr. Seeds told us. Watch out for dangerous cheese.'

Bulmer hobbled to the edge of the hole. 'One, two, three, and here we go!' He flopped over the edge.

Matthew John and Bulmer vanished into the Back of Beyond. The others followed.

Their arms wrapped tightly around the necks of their bats, Matthew John, Joshua Ryan and Emily

Charlotte swooped through the Back of Beyond. The Back of Beyond was an underground maze of twisting tree roots and tumbling waterfalls, lit by glowing blue mosses and shining moonflowers.

'Look!' said Emily Charlotte, picking up a yellow hair ribbon draped over a toadstool. 'This belongs to Annabelle Sue. I'm sure it does. She likes yellow.'

'She must have come this way,' said Matthew John, 'and dropped her ribbon.'

They hovered for a moment, enjoying the scents of jasmine and thyme. The glade was loud with a buzzing sound.

Matthew John took a careful look around, wondering where the buzzing was coming from. Mr. Seeds had warned him to watch out for cheese. 'I don't see any cheese,' he said. 'That sound must be coming from the bees.'

The bees had black and yellow stripes. They were busy collecting nectar from flowers to take back to their nest to make honey. Their nest hung from a tree.

'I smell honey,' said Bulmer, and stuck his tongue into the bees' nest to see if he could find some.

'Bulmer, are you out of your mind?' said Matthew John.

'I like honey,' said Bulmer.

The buzzing grew much louder.

'Ow!' said Bulmer, back winging.

'What's the matter?'

'A bee thtung my tongue,' said Bulmer.

'Serve you right,' said Matthew John.

'My tongue ith swelling up. It feelth like a thponge.'

Angry bees darkened the air. The bees did not like having their honey stolen.

'Quick,' said Matthew John. 'Head for the waterfall.'

The three bat riders put their bats into a steep dive. They headed for the falls far below.

Six thousand furious bees dived after them. The drone of the bees became an angry din.

The roar of the bees swelled.

'We'll be stung to pieces,' said Vesper.

Risking a quick glance over his shoulder, Matthew John saw that the swarm of bees was gaining on them rapidly.

'Faster, Bulmer,' he said. 'You don't want to be stung again.'

'I thould thay not,' said Bulmer.

The din of the bees became louder. The bees came nearer.

'We're not going to make it,' said Emily Charlotte.

'Yes we are,' said Matthew John.

The three bat riders flew their bats through the falling curtain of water.

The bees were baffled by the waterfall, and returned to their nest.

'Thupid beeth,' said Bulmer. 'My tongue hurth.'

The bat riders looked about them. A shimmering

wall of water lay behind them, and a strange cave lay before them.

'This is awesome,' said Smoky.

They had entered a grotto in which a thousand mushrooms shone like blue-white stars.

Suddenly, without warning, all three bats stopped flying in midair. Bells jangled.

'Whath thith?' said Bulmer. 'Why can't I move my wingth?'

Matthew John put out a hand and felt the strands of a net. The net had been strung from one side of the cave to the other. The strands felt soft, and smelled of Yumi fruit. 'We're caught in an invisible net,' he said.

'Who set this net?' mused Joshua Ryan.

They heard someone coming. The footfalls grew louder.

'Ssh!' said Emily Charlotte. She whispered in her bat's ear. 'Vesper, keep still! You'll tangle yourself.'

'Too late,' said Vesper. 'I'm tangled already.'

'Well, well,' said a man's voice, 'and who do we have here?'

Matthew John saw by his uniform that the man was a policeman.

'I'm Matthew John.'

'I'm Joshua Ryan.'

'I'm Emily Charlotte.'

'I'm Constable Boot of the Root Police. You can't just come flying into the Back of Beyond, you know. It's against the law.'

'I'm sorry, Constable Boot,' said Matthew John. 'We didn't mean to do anything wrong. We are looking for a classmate of ours. Her name is Annabelle Sue. She's about my size, with blonde hair. We have been sent to find her. We have to bring her home to her parents. Can you help?'

'You're under arrest,' said Constable Boot.

He reached up and pulled on a strand of the invisible net. The net fell to the floor of the grotto, carrying with it the three trapped bats and their riders.

'Ow!' said Emily Charlotte, bumping her knee on the stone.

'That hurt,' said Vesper.

Constable Boot gathered up the invisible net, bats and riders, and carried them on his back to the police station. He put them in a jail cell. 'As you can see,' he said, 'you're not the first intruder I've arrested today.' He closed the jail cell door and turned the key in the lock.

A roar shook the building.

'That sounds like a lion,' said the constable. 'I shall have to investigate.' He strode out of the station.

In a corner of their jail cell, glowering at them, sat a girl with blonde hair.

'Annabelle Sue!' said Emily Charlotte. 'It's you! Here's your hair ribbon. I found it.'

'We've come to your rescue,' said Joshua Ryan.

'Some rescue,' said Annabelle Sue. 'Maybe I should be rescuing you. You seem to be in more trouble than I am. You are caught up in some kind of net. Why is your bat sticking his tongue out at me?'

'I'm not trying to be rude,' said Bulmer. 'I wath thtung by a bee, you thee.'

'So I'm to be rescued by this bat with a speech problem, and by three tangled up riders? Where are my truffles?'

'Where are your what?' said Joshua Ryan.

Annabelle Sue stood up and put her hand on her hips. She sighed. 'Let me guess. Nobody told you about the truffles.'

'What are truffles?' said Emily Charlotte.

'Truffles,' said Annabelle Sue, tapping her foot on the floor and trying to keep her temper, 'are things to eat. Truffles grow among the roots of the Yumi trees. That's why I'm here in the Back of Beyond. I'm looking for truffles. My Daddy needs truffles for his cooking. He's a chef.'

'We've met him,' said Joshua Ryan. 'He's baking you a pie.'

Annabelle Sue grew excited. 'He is? A Yumi pie?'

'Yes,' said Matthew John. 'He said Yumi pies were your favorite.'

'They are. They taste wonderful straight from the oven,' said Annabelle Sue. 'I must get out of this jail at once.'

'Can you free uth from thith net firsth?' said Bulmer.

'Sure,' said Annabelle Sue. She yanked at the invisible net, and freed the bats and their riders.

'Thanks,' said Matthew John.

'That feels better,' said Joshua Ryan.

'Much better,' said Emily Charlotte.

'Constable Boot has locked the cell door and left the key in the lock,' said Annabelle Sue. 'So how do we get out? I take it you have a plan?'

'We're working on a plan,' said Matthew John.

The beast roared again, much closer. It did sound like a lion.

'You'd better come up with your plan soon,' said Annabelle Sue.

The door burst open.

A huge lion with a yellow mane leaped into the police station.

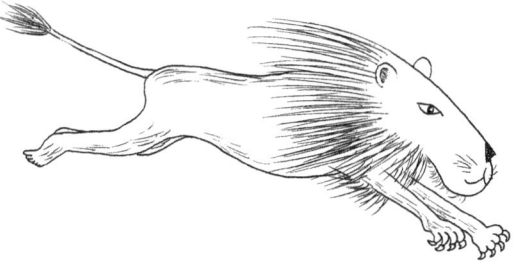

When the cave lion Oomba had smelled sponge cake and raspberries, he had been reminded of another time, not long ago, when he had chased after a different scent. Then it had been the smell of peach milkshake that had intrigued him. Oomba had been chasing a young bat that had fallen to the floor of the cave, and, when a boy had leaped on the bat's back and both boy and bat had taken to the air, Oomba had leaped after them. He had been unable to catch them, lost his balance and tumbled into an underground river. He hadn't drowned, for he knew how to swim, but the river had swept him far out to sea.

To stay afloat, he had paddled for hours. It had been a most annoying experience. To make matters worse, a storm had sprung up, making waves so big that Oomba had got water up his nose. That had made him cross.

He had seen an island and had swum towards it. He had waded ashore. He had shaken himself dry, sending seawater flying. He had felt like having a light snack after his swim. He had eaten sixteen antelopes, three water buffalo and a giraffe, and then, casting about for something for dessert, he had come upon this most delicious smell of sponge cake and raspberries. He had bounded across three valleys, drooling with excitement. The scent had grown stronger and stronger, and now he was arriving at the police station from which the delicious smell was coming. He gave a great roar of savage satisfaction.

You are mine, Sponge Cake and Raspberries!

He leaped into the police station.

The lion skidded across the police station floor, slammed into the outside of the cell, and tried to claw the prisoners through the bars, but could not reach them.

'I know this lion,' said Matthew John. 'It's Oomba, the lion from our cave. He's come to eat us.'

'This is your plan?' said Annabelle Sue. 'We all get eaten by a lion? Next time you plan on rescuing me, don't bother. I can do better by myself.'

Oomba rattled the door of the cell. The cell door shook but did not give way. It was made of steel. The lion became bothered. The lion could see the creatures that smelled of raspberries and sponge cake but could not get at them.

'If you want to eat us, Oomba,' said Matthew John, 'you'll have to unlock the cell door. I bet you don't know how. I bet you have never unlocked a door in your whole life.'

'DOOR!' roared Oomba.

'That's right, Oomba,' said Matthew John. 'The door. The door is the thing with the door handle and the lock. Use your brain, Oomba. The key is in the lock. All you have to do is turn it.'

'KEY!' roared Oomba.

'That's right. Oomba. The key. Nudge the key with your nose,' said Matthew John. 'Go on! You can do it! We're all waiting to be eaten. Just nudge the key with your nose. You remember where your nose is, do you? Your nose is that thing sticking out of the front of your ugly face.'

'NOSE!' roared Oomba.

'Whose side are you on, Matthew John?' asked Annabelle Sue.

'Don't worry,' said Matthew John. 'He's getting the idea.'

Oomba nudged the key with his nose.

'Nudge a bit more, Oomba,' said Matthew John. 'You can do it.'

The key turned.

Click.

The cell door flew open.

Oomba sprang into the cell, his claws extended. His legs became entangled in the invisible net. He tripped and fell on his face.

'Ride with me, Annabelle Sue,' said Matthew

John, and hauled the chef's daughter onto Bulmer's back. All three bats and their riders sprang into the air, wings beating fast, and darted over Oomba's head and out through the open door of the cell. Matthew John pulled the cell door shut and then turned the key in the lock.

'Don't worry, Oomba,' said Matthew John. 'Constable Boot will take good care of you.'

Matthew John, Joshua Ryan and Emily Charlotte flew their bats out of the police station.

'Yahoo!' said Annabelle Sue.

They felt wonderful. They had escaped from the cell. They had got away from the lion. They were free.

Annabelle Sue held on tightly to Matthew John's waist as they zoomed this way and that among the winding and twisting roots of the great Yumi trees.

'Truffles!' cried Annabelle Sue in Matthew John's ear, and she pointed.

Bulmer swooped down so that his riders might help themselves to some truffles.

Annabelle Sue chose three white and three black truffles.

Matthew John had not seen truffles before. They had rough skins, and a wonderful aroma.

'My Daddy's going to be so pleased we found six,' said Annabelle Sue. 'Just what he wanted.'

The riders rode their bats out of the Back of Beyond.

The storm had blown over. The wind had died down. The sun had come out.

They landed outside Chef Wandor's Jelly Belly Restaurant, and Annabelle Sue led the way inside.

Chef Wandor was delighted to see his daughter. 'Annabelle Sue!' he said, and swept her up into the air and swung her round and round his head.

'Daddy! Don't! You'll make me drop the truffles.'

'Truffles? You brought me truffles?' Chef Wandor

gave his little girl a big hug and returned her safely to the ground. 'You did! Six big truffles. You are clever daughter. But you gave me big fright, disappearing down that hole into the Back of Beyond. You must never do that again.'

'I won't, Daddy. I promise,' said Annabelle Sue.

'You found daughter,' said Chef Wandor to the bat riders. 'You are incredible. You are magnificent. I give you big hugs.'

Annabelle Sue's Mummy came out of the kitchen carrying a Yumi pie, hot from the oven. She put the pie on the table.

'Oh, Mummy,' said Annabelle Sue. She was anxious to bring her mother up to date with her adventures. 'Constable Boot put me in jail and a lion came and roared but we flew away just in time and I found some truffles and the bat riders are Matthew John, Joshua Ryan and Emily Charlotte, and their bats are Bulmer, Smoky and Vesper.'

'I missed you too,' her mother said, and gave her girl a big embrace. She turned to the bat riders. 'Thank you for finding Annabelle Sue and for bringing her home,' she said.

'You're most welcome,' said Matthew John.

Chef Wandor handed out slices of Yumi pie and for a while nobody said anything because they were too busy eating.

'Here are a dozen more Yumi pies for you to take back with you,' said the chef.

'I want to go with them. I want to see their bat cave,' said Annabelle Sue.

'Why not?' said Chef Wandor.

'We know she will be safe with you,' said Annabelle Sue's mother quietly to Emily Charlotte.

'I wish I had a bat,' said Annabelle Sue.

Matthew John, Annabelle Sue, Joshua Ryan and Emily Charlotte flew back across the sea.

They landed in Mr. Seeds's garden.

'Mr. Seeds! We have a pie for you.'

Mr. Seeds wheeled his chair out of his front door. 'What a fine gift. I am most grateful.'

'Why did you warn us to beware of cheese?' asked Matthew John.

'I warned you to beware of bees, not cheese.'

'Beeth,' said Bulmer. 'Thath what you thaid.'

'Wish we could stay, Mr. Seeds, but we have to report back to our squadron,' said Matthew John.

They left Mr. Seeds's house, waved goodbye to him, and flew to the street where Matthew John lived.

Joshua Ryan and Emily Charlotte gave their parents Yumi pies.

Matthew John took Annabelle Sue to meet his Mummy and Daddy. 'She's a friend from school. Her father runs a restaurant.'

'How nice to meet you,' said Mummy.

'We've brought this pie for you,' said Annabelle Sue.

'My, oh my,' said Mummy. 'The pie is still warm. Thank you so much.'

'It was brave of you to fly a mission during a storm,' said Daddy. 'I'm proud of you, Matthew John.'

'Thanks, Dad. I'm afraid we can't stay. We have to

report back to our squadron leader.'

They took off. They flew in triangular formation. They swooped into the cave where the bats and their riders lived.

The other bat riders gave a rousing cheer when they saw Annabelle Sue seated safely behind Matthew John on Bulmer's back.

They landed in the squadron leader's cavern and dismounted. Bulmer, Smoky and Vesper flew up to the ceiling and hung there upside down, their ears cocked to hear what their riders were saying.

'Squadron leader,' said Matthew John. 'This is Annabelle Sue.'

'I'm glad to see you safe,' said the squadron leader.

'These Yumi pies are a present for the squadron,' said Annabelle Sue. 'They are from my Mummy and Daddy.'

'Thanks. They smell wonderful.'

'I want to be a bat rider,' said Annabelle Sue, 'but I haven't got a bat.'

'We can do something about that,' said the squadron leader, and turned back to Matthew John. 'How did you find her?'

Matthew John told of their adventure in the Back of Beyond.

'You met Oomba the lion?' said the squadron leader. 'I had wondered what had become of that creature. Well, I am so glad you came to no harm in the end. I congratulate all of you. Matthew John, your first mission has been a success, and I have news. I have grown too big and heavy to ride my bat Hula. I can no longer be a bat rider.' She looked away.

'You must be sad,' said Emily Charlotte, 'and Hula must be sad, too.'

'Hula is sad, but she won't be sad for long,' said the squadron leader. 'While you were away rescuing Annabelle Sue, I told the squadron I was stepping down and asked them to choose someone else to be squadron leader and to take my place. They took a vote and they chose you for their next squadron leader, Matthew John.'

'Me?' said Matthew John. 'The bat riders chose me to be squadron leader? But I'm so small.'

'They chose you because of your bravery. You flew out into the storm and you inspired your friends to do the same.'

'I nearly got us all eaten by a lion,' said Matthew John.

'I dare say that's true. Nobody can force you to be squadron leader. It's up to you. Do you want to be?'

'Emily Charlotte?' said Matthew John. 'What do you think? They should have chosen you or Joshua Ryan to be squadron leader.'

'I think you should say yes,' said Emily Charlotte.

'Go for it,' said Joshua Ryan. 'Bulmer tells us you want to be squadron leader. This is your chance.'

'Take the job, kid,' said Bulmer.

The bat Hula flew down from the ceiling and flopped onto the cave floor beside Annabelle Sue. 'Would you like to be my rider, Annabelle Sue?' asked Hula.

'May I?' Annabelle Sue asked, looking up at Hula's old rider.

The retiring squadron leader nodded.

Annabelle Sue climbed onto Hula's back.

'Hang on tight,' said Hula, and launched herself.

'I'm flying!' said Annabelle Sue. 'Look at me! I'm a bat rider!'

'And I'm your squadron leader,' said Matthew John.

CHAPTER IV

Armando's Dream

THE QUEEN BEE stared at Matthew John. 'Your bat Bulmer helped himself to my honey?' she said. 'What was he thinking?'

'I'm afraid Bulmer doesn't think much,' said Matthew John, rubbing the back of his neck. 'Most of the time, he just does whatever comes into his head.'

'That's no excuse, squadron leader,' said the queen. 'As a punishment, I shall tell my bees not to visit your Yumi trees. Put one hand on your chest, the other hand behind your back, and bow.'

'Yes, your majesty,' said Matthew John. He stood and bowed respectfully to the queen.

'How did I do?' asked Matthew John, after the queen had gone.

'Good thing she didn't see me up here hanging by my feet from the ceiling,' said Bulmer.

'Next time you want to eat something, Bulmer, ask me first.'

'I'll try to remember,' said Bulmer, and dropped down to join Matthew John at the edge of the ledge overlooking the cavern where the bats and their riders lived.

'Want to go for a spin?' asked Bulmer.

'Yes,' said Matthew John.

Matthew John climbed onto Bulmer's back and wrapped his arms round Bulmer's neck. Bulmer's brown fur felt warm, soft and comfortable. Bulmer was Matthew John's best friend.

'Let's go and pick some Yumi fruit,' said Matthew John.

'Whooee!' said Bulmer, and flopped over the edge. He spread his leathery wings. He swooped through the cave. He made the hammocks of the other bat riders swing. 'Let's do a tail slide,' he said.

'Do a what?' asked Matthew John.

'I'll show you,' said Bulmer, and flew straight up towards the cave ceiling. He stalled, and then fell backward. He turned head over tail.

'Yikes!' cried Matthew John.

Bulmer spread his wings wide. He pulled out of his dive. He flew low over the floor. A group of baby bats were playing in the glowing moss. They fled in alarm.

'What are you doing?' said Matthew John.

'I'm doing whatever comes into my head,' said Bulmer.

'You overheard what I said,' said Matthew John.

'I have big ears,' said Bulmer.

'I love you, Bulmer,' said Matthew John. 'You're the best bat on the planet.'

'I love you too, Matthew John,' said Bulmer. 'How about a barrel roll?'

'We had better pick some Yumi fruit.'

'Okay,' said Bulmer. 'Here we go!'

They zoomed out of the cave. They flew up to the top of a mile-high Yumi tree. They sailed into a treetop garden and crashed into a pond.

'Oops,' said Bulmer. 'Sorry about that. Lucky I missed the swans.'

The swans grabbed Matthew John's shirt and Bulmer's wings with their beaks, and dragged the pair ashore. They were used to rescuing Matthew John and Bulmer, for they had done it before.

'Thanks,' said Bulmer.

Matthew John shook himself and sent water flying. 'We've come to pick some Yumi fruit to give to Mr. Seeds.'

'There are no fruit to pick,' said the mother swan.

'No Yumi fruit, no Yumi fruit, no Yumi fruit,' said the baby swans.

Matthew John frowned. 'There are always Yumi fruit,' he said.

'Not any more, not any more, not any more,' said the baby swans.

The tree spoke in a deep, slow voice. 'I'm afraid the little swans are right,' he said, wiping his eye with a twiggy hand. 'Without the help of the bees,' he went on, 'my flowers can't turn into fruit. Without fruit, there won't be any more Yumi trees. That is the truth, or my name is not Boris.'

'Cheer up, Boris,' said Matthew John. He patted the tree's trunk. 'I'll find a way to turn your flowers into fruit. I'll call my boss.' He reached in his pocket for his bat rider phone. 'Wing commander?' he said into the phone.

'Who are you?' said the wing commander.

'My name is Matthew John. I'm the new squadron leader in charge of Number Five Squadron. The bees won't change the flowers into fruit, wing commander. There will be no more Yumi fruit.'

'We are doomed,' said the wing commander. 'Bat riders are supposed to harvest the Yumi fruit. Without Yumi fruit, there will be no more Yumi trees. This is a crisis, and I can't think what to do. I give up. I quit. I am no longer your wing commander. Goodbye.'

The phone went dead.

Matthew John shook his head. He put his phone back in his pocket. 'I wish I were wing commander,' he said, 'I wouldn't give up so easily, but I'm only a squadron leader. There must be some way to save our planet. I'll go and see Mr. Seeds. Mr. Seeds is the wisest man I know.'

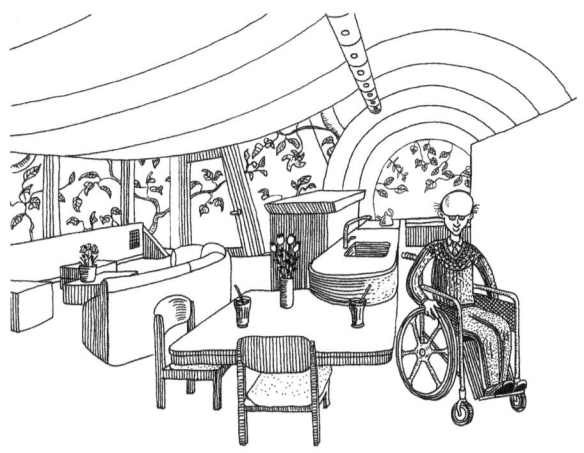

'No bees?' said Mr. Seeds.
'What should we do?' asked Matthew John.

Mr. Seeds poured grape juice onto a scoop of ice cream in his blender. He pushed the LIQUIFY button. He poured the frothy mixture into three glasses. 'Try this. It's called a purple cow ice cream soda. Help yourself to straws.'

'It's yummy,' said Matthew John, sucking it up.

'It makes me shiver,' said Bulmer.

'You should go and talk to the moon moths,' said Mr. Seeds. 'The moon moths can turn flowers into fruit.'

There was a long silence while they enjoyed their purple cow ice cream sodas.

Matthew John sucked up the last of his drink. He washed out the three empty glasses under the tap in the kitchen sink, and put the straws in the recycling bin.

'I've never met any moon moths,' he said. 'Where do they live?'

'The moon moths live on the moon,' said Mr. Seeds. 'You must go to the moon if you want to find them. Be careful. Don't eat the moon pies. Moon pies make you forgetful.'

'What does forgetful mean?'

'You can't remember things.'

'How do we get to the moon?'

'You fly as fast as you can.'

'Thank you, Mr. Seeds,' said Matthew John.

'Good luck, Matthew John,' said Mr. Seeds.

Matthew John and Bulmer went out into the garden.

Matthew John climbed onto Bulmer's back. He

used his bat rider phone to speak with his friends Joshua Ryan, Emily Charlotte and Annabelle Sue.

'We're off to the moon,' he said. 'Want to come?'

'Yes, please,' said Joshua Ryan. 'My bat Smoky wants to go to the moon.'

'We'll come,' said Emily Charlotte. 'My bat Vesper says it will be dangerous.'

'My bat Hula loves danger,' said Annabelle Sue, 'and so do I.'

'Meet me at my house in five minutes,' said Matthew John, 'and don't forget to tell your parents where you are going.'

Bulmer flew Matthew John home.

Matthew John's mother looked worried. 'Are you sure it's safe to go on a moon mission?' she asked.

'Mr. Seeds says we must. He says we have to ask the moon moths for help.'

'I wish you well,' said Daddy. 'Your mother and I would come with you if we could.'

'I wish it were possible,' said Matthew John, 'but you are too big and heavy to ride on the backs of bats.'

'I know,' said Daddy sadly.

Matthew John pumped his fist at the sky. 'To the moon!' he cried.

The four riders rode their bats high up into the sky.

'Mr. Seeds says we mustn't eat the moon pies,' said Matthew John. 'Is everybody ready?'

'Ready,' said Joshua Ryan.

'Ready,' said Emily Charlotte.

'Ready,' said Annabelle Sue.

'Go!'

'Eep! Eep!' cried Bulmer.

Bang! Bang! Bang! Bang!

They burst through the sound barrier.

'I see stars!' said Emily Charlotte.

'My nose is heating up,' said Bulmer.

'My nose is smoking,' said Smoky.

'It's the friction,' said Vesper. 'We are burning up in the moon's atmosphere. I expect we'll explode.'

'I see the moon!' said Joshua Ryan, excitedly.

'Zigzag!' said Matthew John. 'Try to slow down.'

They zigged between two moon mountains.

They zagged into a moon canyon.

They swooped down towards the surface.

'Uh-oh,' said Bulmer. 'I'm not good at landings.'

'We need something soft to break our fall,' said Emily Charlotte.

'Head for that circus tent,' said Matthew John.

Phut! Phut! Phut! Phut!

They made four holes in the striped canvas.

Inside the tent, the bats spread their wings wide and flew in a circle over the heads of the circus audience.

'All the way from the planet of the Yumi trees, ladies and gentlemen,' bellowed the lion tamer, pretending that the arrival of four young people riding bats was part of his show, 'let's hear it for the four daring bat riders!'

The audience clapped.

'Why are the bat riders on fire?' asked a child.

On fire?

Trailing smoke, Matthew John and his friends dived into a water tank.

There was a loud hiss.

A cloud of steam rose from the tank.

A circus performer, the Amazing Dingbat, leapt from the pool and ran out of the tent, followed by sixteen singing penguins.

The audience cheered.

Matthew John surfaced. 'Anyone hurt?' he asked.

'Vesper and I are just fine,' said Emily Charlotte.

'Smoky and I are okay, too,' said Joshua Ryan, 'just a little singed around the edges.'

'Hula and I are getting our breath back,' said Annabelle Sue, patting her bat. 'So this is what you do on missions? You burst into flames and then plunge into pools filled with penguins?' She had never been on a mission before.

'Every mission is different,' said Matthew John. 'How about you, Bulmer?' he went on. 'Are you all right?'

'I'm still alive,' said Bulmer, feeling his burnt nose. 'I think.'

Armando the lion tamer twirled his moustaches. He raised his top hat. He bowed to the four bat riders and their bats as they climbed out of the pool. 'It is I, the great Armando, the fearless lion tamer, who speaks,' he said. 'Welcome to the Loony Moon Circus!'

'I'm Matthew John. We are pleased to be here. I'm sorry we made holes in your tent.'

'I, the fearless Armando, forgive you,' said

Armando. 'Here are your ringside seats. Enjoy the show. I thrill you to pieces.'

'Thanks, Armando,' said Matthew John.

Armando put his hat back on his head and strode into the middle of the ring. 'Ladies and gentlemen, I present to you: Dan Didgeridoo and Matilda the Kangaroo.'

There was a drum roll.

A kangaroo came bounding into the ring, followed by a long-legged man wearing a brown hat decorated with corks dangling from strings.

Matthew John rubbed himself dry with a circus towel while the kangaroo danced and the band played 'Waltzing Matilda.'

Clowns sat on balloons. The bangs of the bursting balloons were so loud that people in the audience put their hands over their ears.

The Zamboni family made a human pyramid. Their youngest daughter climbed up onto the heads of her brothers and sisters, and balanced there, twirling an umbrella on her nose.

A cage rolled into the ring. Inside the cage was a lion. The lion pushed open the door of the cage. The lion walked stiffly out onto the sandy floor of the arena.

The lion tamer, armed with a wooden chair in one hand and a whip in the other, approached the lion.

'Never fear,' he bellowed. 'The brave Armando, the daring lion tamer, is here.' He cracked his whip at the lion.

The lion stood on two legs. The lion clawed at the air with its front paws.

Armando advanced towards the lion, holding the chair out in front of him.

The lion snarled and swiped at the chair with one of its paws. The chair fell apart.

The audience gasped.

Armando threw aside the broken chair and his whip, and flung himself on the lion. He fought the lion with his bare hands. He and the lion rolled over and over in the sand.

'Bad lion!' said Armando. His voice sounded muffled. His head was inside the lion's mouth.

'We must save him,' said Matthew John, and ran to the rescue of Armando.

Emily Charlotte, Joshua Ryan and Annabelle Sue ran to help.

Annabelle Sue grabbed the lion's tail and pulled.

Joshua Ryan pried open the lion's jaws.

Matthew John dragged Armando out of the lion's mouth.

Annabelle Sue and Emily Charlotte stuffed the lion back into its cage.

Matthew John slammed and fastened the cage door.

The audience cheered, clapped and blew whistles.

Armando jumped to his feet. 'That's all for now, folks!' he bellowed. 'Our next performance is at seven.'

The audience filed out of the tent, chattering happily.

When the last member of the audience had left, Armando opened the cage door. He took a remote control from his pocket. He pressed ROAR. The lion gave a hiccup. He pressed WALK. The lion whirred and tried to stand up. It fell over onto its side. 'What have you done to my lion?' he said.

'I'm so sorry, Armando,' said Matthew John. 'We thought it was a real lion.'

'A real lion?' said Armando. 'You think I would wrestle with a real lion? You think I would put my head inside the mouth of a real lion?'

'You said you were a daring lion-tamer,' said Annabelle Sue, her eyes blazing.

'I was once,' said Armando. He seated himself on the edge of the ring. He mopped his forehead with a big spotted handkerchief. 'I went to lion tamer school. I was given my own lion. He was a fine lion. He had a big yellow mane, six toes on his back paws, and a tail that stuck out straight behind. I taught him to stand on his hind legs. I taught him to count up to three. I taught him to jump through a hoop. We were buddies, my lion and I. We were this close.' Armando pinched his thumb and forefinger together to show how much he had loved his lion.

'What happened?' asked Matthew John.

'My classmates became afraid that my lion and I were going to win the class prize,' said Armando. 'They smuggled my lion away in middle of night. They released my lion somewhere in the forest. I searched and searched, but I never saw my lion again.' Armando dabbed at his eyes.

'That was sad,' said Matthew John. 'What did you do?'

'I ran away. I came here, to moon. I join circus. There are no lions on moon, so I built this robot lion for my act,' said Armando, 'and now look at my robot lion! My robot lion can't even stand up without falling over.'

'I'll fix your robot lion for you,' said Matthew John.

Armando looked Matthew John in the eye. He twisted his handkerchief in his hands. 'In my heart,' he said quietly, 'it is not the robot lion that I truly want. It is my real lion. I miss my real lion so much. I ask myself: Where is my real lion now? Is he still lost in the forest? What is my real lion doing?'

On the planet of the Yumi trees, Armando's real lion had enjoyed a light breakfast of twenty-three springboks, nineteen deer, and a warthog. Now he was having a pleasant after-breakfast swim in the smoking lake of Mount Boom. The lake water had tickly bubbles. Oomba liked bubbles.

The hot water made him feel lazy. The steam rising from the lake reminded him of the days of his youth. His trainer Armando had often given him a bath. Armando had scrubbed his back with a long-handled brush. He sighed. He missed Armando. He wondered if he would ever see his trainer again.

Oomba could hear the mountain rumbling beneath him. Oomba was pleased that the mountain was purring. He thought it must be a happy mountain. Nobody had ever told Oomba about volcanoes.

The water in the crater grew hot.

Oomba swam out to the middle of the lake. He floated on his back, looking up at the sky. His yellow mane spread out around him in the water. He felt at peace with the world. The warthog had been delicious.

Deep beneath the lake, the mountain trembled. Hidden underground chambers filled to bursting. Pressure grew and grew.

Oomba floated lazily on his back, smiling up at the moon. He had no idea what was about to happen.

Boom!

The mountain blew up. The eruption lifted the lake and the lion high into the air.

Oomba tumbled head over tail through space and hit the moon's atmosphere. He fell towards the surface.

He saw a herd of grazing moon beasts. He bared his teeth.

He landed on the back of the largest of the beasts, and ate it.

He licked his lips. Moon beast tasted even better than warthog. Now what he wanted was something for dessert. He sniffed the air. He smelled purple cow ice cream soda. The tempting smell was coming from a striped tent. He bounded across the moonscape towards the tent. Every bound sent him soaring high above the ground. On his final bound he ripped through the canvas of the tent and landed on all fours in the middle of the circus ring.

He roared with excitement. Purple cow ice cream soda, he thought, you are mine, all mine.

The audience for the seven o'clock show was impressed by the dramatic arrival of the lion, and gave a great cheer. Armando the lion tamer was impressed, too. Evidently his robot lion had been improved, for it now looked like a real lion, leapt like a real lion, and roared like a real lion. Matthew John had repaired the robot lion well.

The lion tamer walked forward, cracking his whip.

He was astonished when the robot lion stood up on its hind legs, placed its front paws on Armando's shoulders, and licked his face.

Armando's eyes grew as big and round as saucers.

This was not a robot lion!

This was a real lion.

And not just any old real lion, he thought. This is the real lion I trained at lion tamer school.

'Oomba?' he said, staring into the lion's eyes. 'Oomba, my old friend. You have found me?

'AR!' roared Oomba.

'Ah, it is good to see you, buddy,' said Armando, and patted the lion's neck.

'MAN!' roared Oomba.

'Man, oh man!' said Armando, 'am I pleased to see you!'

'DO!' roared Oomba.

'Don't mention it, Oomba,' said Armando. 'I've missed you, too. I can't tell you how much it means to me to have you slobbering all over my face. You are a dear, dear lion.'

At that moment, Matthew John entered the ring with the robot lion trotting at his heels.

'I can't stop the tail wagging,' said Matthew John, 'but I have got the legs working, and listen to this.' He pressed the ROAR button on the remote.

The robot lion roared.

Oomba ground his teeth. Another lion had invaded *his* territory! His hair stood on end. He roared back.

The crowd stamped their feet. This was a really good circus. It had two lions.

Matthew John stood very still, staring at the real lion. He clenched his fist. He knew this lion, and he did not like the hungry look he saw in the lion's eyes.

Matthew John smelled of purple cow ice cream soda.

He had to escape. But how could he?

'You know my Oomba?' asked Armando, raising his eyebrows.

'We have met before,' said Matthew John, carefully. He did not say that Oomba had tried to eat him. Matthew John was in great danger. He needed his bat, Bulmer, to fly him to safety. 'Bulmer?' he said softly. 'Are you there?'

There was no answer.

Matthew John risked a quick glance up at the trapeze. He saw no bats hanging there.

'Are any of the other bat riders about? Joshua Ryan? Emily Charlotte? Annabelle Sue?'

Armando shook his head.

Matthew John swallowed.

The tip of Oomba's tail flicked from side to side.

The lion was about to spring, and Armando would not be able to stop him.

Matthew John gnawed his knuckles. Where were his friends?

Matthew John's friends were hard at work searching throughout the circus, trying to find Bulmer.

Bulmer was in the circus kitchen, eyeing the moon pies. The pies were straight out of the oven.

'They smell wonderful,' said Bulmer, gazing at the pies. He licked his lips. 'Matthew John told me not to eat them. He said that if you bite into a moon pie, you go loony. You forget who you are. You forget who your friends are. You forget all about everything. The pastry looks flaky.'

'It is,' said Dan Didgeridoo, taking a moon pie from the table and biting into it. Juice dribbled down his chin.

'Does eating moon pie really make you forget things?' asked Bulmer.

'Forget what?' said Dan Didgeridoo, popping a piece of moon pie into the mouth of his kangaroo.

'I want to forget that I stole some honey and made the queen bee angry,' said Bulmer.

'Have a pie,' said Dan.

'Thanks, Dan,' said Bulmer and popped a moon pie into his mouth.

'Who's Dan?' asked Dan.

Bulmer frowned. 'Uh. I don't know. Somebody I had to thank, I think.'

'Who are you?' asked Dan.

'No idea,' said Bulmer. He saw himself in a mirror. 'Wow! I have wings.'

Bulmer popped a second moon pie in his mouth and hobbled out of the kitchen. Whatever kind of creature he was, he was terribly bad at walking. He looked down. His legs were part of his wings! How weird was that?

'Bulmer,' said Emily Charlotte. 'We've been looking everywhere for you.'

Bulmer did not answer. The moon pies had made him forget who Emily Charlotte was. He stretched his wings out to see what they looked like. They were made of skin! Neat! The skin was stretched tight over long, thin bones.

These are my wings, he thought. I wonder if I can make them flap.

He lurched into the air.

'Bulmer!' said Emily Charlotte. 'Come back!'

Bulmer paid no attention.

'Something is wrong,' said Emily Charlotte. 'I don't think Bulmer can hear me.'

'Bulmer has lost his mind,' said Emily Charlotte's bat Vesper. 'He never had much of a mind to begin with.'

'We had better keep an eye on him, if that's the case,' said Joshua Ryan, 'in case he does something foolish.'

'He's flying jerkily,' said Joshua Ryan's bat

Smoky. 'I think he's forgotten how to flap his wings.'

'Ah,' said Annabelle Sue. 'This must be the exciting part of our mission. We chase a loony bat who has forgotten who he is.'

'He's vanishing into the fog,' said Hula.

'Quick!' cried Joshua Ryan. 'After him!'

Joshua Ryan, Emily Charlotte, and Annabelle Sue mounted their bats and followed Bulmer into the fog.

A palace loomed, shadowy and strange.

'Bulmer, watch out!' cried Joshua Ryan.

Bulmer slammed into the palace roof, bounced, skidded over the tiles, and fell through a skylight.

'Bulmer has crashed,' said Emily Charlotte. 'I wish Matthew John were here. Where is he, I wonder?'

Matthew John was in the circus ring watching the real lion Oomba gather himself to pounce.

Matthew John had thought of a way to escape. He would leap onto the back of the robot lion.

Oomba sprang at Matthew John.

Matthew John vaulted onto the back of the robot lion. He hit the GIANT LEAP button on the remote.

The robot lion made a giant leap. He sprang into the air and sailed over Oomba's head.

Matthew John pressed the button for RUN FAST.

The robot lion ran fast. It rushed out of the tent with Matthew John clinging to its back. It tore through a forest of flaming moon trees and across a moon swamp.

Matthew John looked over his shoulder.

Oomba was bounding in pursuit, and he was gaining.

Matthew John pressed the button for RUN EVEN FASTER. The robot lion made a clicking sound and then went twice as fast as before.

Matthew John hung on tightly. Could he steer? He twisted the head of the robot lion to the left.

The robot lion swerved to the left. The robot lion pelted through a field of glowing white moonflowers, sending petals flying.

Matthew John glanced back at Oomba.

Oomba was closer.

Matthew John pressed the button for RUN AS FAST AS YOU CAN.

The robot lion made a grinding sound and began to run as fast as it could. The robot lion's legs banged up and down.

A red light came on saying LOW BATTERY.

Uh-oh, thought Matthew John, and twisted the robot lion's head sharply to the right, steering for a big building that looked like a palace. The palace stood shrouded in fog.

A tunnel led down into the palace basement.

The robot lion charged into the basement.

It was dark in the basement.

Something grabbed Matthew John and dragged him from the back of the robot lion.

Matthew John felt the slippery tendrils of a strangling moon plant curling around his arms and legs. Matthew John fought to free himself, but the plant would not let go.

As he struggled with the moon plant, Matthew John heard the robot lion rattle out of the other end of the basement, and charge off into the distance. Moments later, he heard Oomba the real lion rush by in hot pursuit.

The sounds of the real lion chasing the robot lion grew fainter and fainter.

Matthew John could not hear them any more.

He was alone in the dark.

'Help!' cried Matthew John. 'I'm being eaten!'

His cry echoed throughout the basement.

'Eaten!' said the echo.

'I need help!' he shouted.

'Help!' said the echo.

'Is there anybody out there?' he shouted. 'Is there anybody I know?'

'No,' said the echo.

The plant wrapped its tendrils more tightly around him. Soon Matthew John could not move at all. He could not even reach the phone in his pocket.

Where were his fellow bat riders? Where were Joshua Ryan, Emily Charlotte and Annabelle Sue?

Where was his bat Bulmer?

The emperor of the moths leaned forward in his throne. 'Two lions, you say? One chasing the other?'

'Yes, your Imperial Magnificence,' said the chamberlain. 'They flattened your moonflowers.'

'We need those moonflowers,' said the emperor.

A monster fell through the palace skylight and landed on the marble floor of the Imperial Court with a thud.

The courtiers rose into the air in a flutter of powdered wings, uttering cries of alarm.

Four hundred members of the emperor's guard held the monster firmly.

'Who are you?' said the emperor, frowning at the beast.

'I have no idea,' said Bulmer.

'What is the last thing you remember?' asked the emperor.

'Eating moon pies,' said Bulmer.

The emperor smiled. 'Moon pies make one forgetful. What kind of monster are you?'

'He's a bat,' said Joshua Ryan, guiding his bat Smoky down to land on the marble floor.

'He has come all the way from the Planet of the Yumi trees,' said Emily Charlotte, guiding her bat Vesper down to join him. 'And so have we.'

Annabelle Sue landed her bat Hula right beside the throne. 'If you want to know who we are,' she whispered in the emperor's ear, 'this is Joshua Ryan, this is Emily Charlotte, and my name is Annabelle Sue. We are bat riders.'

'If you are bat riders,' said the emperor, frowning, 'then where is the rider of this fourth bat?'

'We left him at the circus trying to fix a robot lion,' said Annabelle Sue.

Joshua Ryan took his bat rider phone from his pocket and called Matthew John.

They all heard the faint sound of Matthew John's ringtone, and looked at one another in surprise. The ringtone seemed to be coming from beneath their feet. Matthew John's phone was ringing somewhere in the palace basement.

'Why does he not answer?' said Joshua Ryan.

'He's in trouble,' said Emily Charlotte.

'Release the prisoner,' said the emperor, 'and follow me. We shall find your missing rider.'

They rode with the emperor down moving stairs

and descended to the basement of the palace.

'I hope we find Matthew John,' said Emily Charlotte.

'You hope we find who?' asked Bulmer.

Matthew John could not answer his phone because the moon plant would not let him.

If I don't get help soon, he thought, I shall choke.

He heard voices in the distance.

'I think the sound of the phone is coming from here,' said a voice that might be Emily Charlotte.

A moon plant tendril slid inside Matthew John's mouth.

'Immee, Madue Joon!' shouted Matthew John, trying to tell his friends that it was him, Matthew John. 'Immover ear,' he said, trying to say that he was over here. Bats had keen hearing, and used their ears to find their way about in the dark. He felt sure they would hear him.

'Smoky says he can hear somebody shouting,' said a voice that might be Joshua Ryan, 'but he doesn't know who it is. He says the person is speaking some strange language.'

The moon plant tendril wound itself around Matthew John's tongue.

'Eyenee helanfast!' shouted Matthew John, trying to say that he needed help, and fast.

'He can't speak,' said a voice that was definitely Annabelle Sue. 'This is not a mission. It's a disaster.'

'Eyebee attackle bella hooey!' shouted Matthew John, trying to say he was being attacked and that they had better hurry.

'Quickly, bat riders,' said Joshua Ryan. 'This way!'

Joshua Ryan, Emily Charlotte and Annabelle Sue dashed to free Matthew John from the moon plant.

They tore him free.

They dragged him before the emperor.

'This is our squadron leader,' said Joshua Ryan. 'Matthew John, this is the emperor of the moon moths. He led us to you.'

Matthew John spat a bit of moon plant from his mouth. 'Emperor,' he said. 'Thank you for your help.' It felt good to have his voice back. The emperor was as big as Matthew John's fist, splendidly dressed in golden fur decorated with white and black eyespots.

'My empire is in trouble,' said the emperor. 'Lions have destroyed our moonflowers. I have ten thousand children who will starve if I do not find fresh flowers for them to feed on.'

'We have fresh flowers,' said Matthew John.

The emperor looked hopeful. 'You do? You will allow my ten thousand children visit the flowers on your planet of the Yumi trees?' he said.

'We shall welcome it,' said Matthew John. 'There are plenty of Yumi flowers for them to visit. Will you come along with them? There is someone back at home I should like you to meet.'

'Does she have ten thousand children?' said the emperor.

'Yes, she does,' said Matthew John.

'Good,' said the emperor, and turned to his chamberlain. 'Bring me my shuttle. Bring the children. Tell them I have found flowers for them to visit,' he said.

The emperor's shuttle took off from the moon, passed swiftly and silently through space, and landed on the planet of the Yumi trees just outside the home of Mr. Seeds.

The sun was setting, and the air was heavy with the scent of Yumi flowers.

The emperor climbed out of his shuttle, followed by his ten thousand children, who rose in a great cloud of softly beating wings and disappeared among the treetops to visit the Yumi flowers and to feed upon their nectar.

Matthew John and his friends stepped from the shuttle.

'It feels good to be home,' said Joshua Ryan's bat Smoky.

Mr. Seeds, who had invited the queen of the bees to tea, beckoned to them.

'I found the moon moths, Mr. Seeds,' said Matthew John. 'I have brought you their emperor.'

'Emperor of the Moths,' said Mr. Seeds, 'may I introduce the Queen of the Bees?'

The emperor moth fluttered his wings and turned pink. 'Enchanted to meet you,' he said to the queen.

The queen bee looked him over. 'The pleasure is mine,' she said, and bit him on the nose.

It was love at first bite.

The queen and the emperor made a deal. The bees would visit the Yumi flowers in the daytime, and the moths would visit the Yumi flowers during the night. That way, all of the Yumi flowers would turn into fruit.

The wing commander arrived, riding on his bat Prang. 'A successful mission, squadron leader,' he said, and handed Matthew John his flying goggles. 'I won't be needing these now,' he said. 'You are the new wing commander, Matthew John.'

'Me?' said Matthew John, surprised.

'While you were away, all of the bats in my squadron and all of the bats in your squadron decided that you should take my place and be the new wing commander.'

'I'm not sure I deserve to be a wing commander,' said Matthew John. 'I was nearly throttled by a moon plant, and my friends had to save me.'

'You saved the planet,' said the wing commander. 'Isn't that right, Prang?'

'That's what he did,' said the wing commander's bat Prang. 'He saved us all, even though he is small.'

'Take the job,' said Joshua Ryan.

'Go for it,' said Emily Charlotte.

'You and your barmy bat,' said Annabelle Sue.

'Put the goggles on, kid,' said Bulmer.

'Bulmer! You remember me?' said Matthew John.

Bulmer stared at him. 'Remember who?' he asked.

Matthew John's face fell.

Bulmer grinned. 'Just kidding, Matthew John,' he said. 'Go on. Put on those goggles.'

Matthew John put the goggles on. He was a wing commander! He could not believe it. He was very small to be a wing commander. He would have to work hard to earn the respect of his two squadrons.

The parents of the bat riders hurried over to welcome back their sons and daughters.

'I was worried about you,' said Matthew John's mother.

'There was no need to worry,' said Matthew John, sliding the goggles up onto his forehead. 'The mission was easy.'

'As easy as pie,' said Bulmer.

'Good thing they don't have lions on the moon,' said Matthew John's Daddy.

'They do now,' said Matthew John. He pulled the flying goggles back down over his eyes, and looked up at the moon. Through a gaping hole in the roof of the circus tent, Matthew John could see Armando.

So powerful were the wing commander's goggles, Matthew John could see a tear of joy running down Armando's cheek.

Armando was tugging at his moustaches and gazing fondly down at his old friend Oomba. The beast he loved so much, and had not seen in years, lay sleeping beside the robot lion on the warm sand of the circus ring.

Armando's lion had come back! At long last, Armando was what he had always wanted to be, a real lion tamer with a real lion.

CHAPTER V

Kiti and the Cardboard Box

MATTHEW JOHN hopped onto Prang's back. It was odd to be sitting on the back of a strange bat. He gripped Prang's pale fur with his hands. 'Let's go,' he said, squeezing Prang's sides with his knees. Wings beating, they left the cave where the bat riders lived. Mount Boom erupted. They flew through smoke.

Flaming bombs of red-hot rock fell from the sky.

'I knew this was a bad idea,' said Prang. 'Are you sure you can't find some other bat to ride?'

'It has to be you, Prang,' said Matthew John. 'I trust you. You flew all those missions with your wing commander before he retired.'

'We attended parades and had inspections,' said Prang. 'The wing commander wore his medals.'

'I don't have any medals,' said Matthew John. 'That's my home down there, the house with the red roof. Would you please land on the lawn? I want to tell my parents where I am going. Are you any good at landing? Bulmer crashes all the time.'

'I know how to land,' said Prang, and he landed.

'You've changed your bat,' said Daddy.

'This is Prang,' said Matthew John. 'Bulmer is lost and Prang is going to help me find him.'

'Pleased to meet you, Prang,' said Mummy. 'I do hope nothing serious has happened to Bulmer.'

'Don't worry, Mum,' said Matthew John. 'He's probably crashed somewhere. You know Bulmer. Prang and I will find him. Prang has flown hundreds of missions. Haven't you, Prang?'

'I like the marching bands best,' said Prang, 'and the saluting. Would you like to see me salute?'

'Perhaps another time,' said Mummy. 'I know you must be anxious to start your mission.'

A strange wail came from the forest of mile-high Yumi trees.

Prang's eyes widened. 'What was that?' he asked.

'Sounds like trouble,' said Matthew John. 'We had better go and find out what's wrong. See you later, Mum. Bye, Dad.'

'Wish we could come,' said Daddy. Grown-ups were too heavy to ride on the backs of bats.

'I shall miss you both,' said Matthew John. 'Chocks away, Prang!'

Matthew John and Prang leapt from the ground and flew up through swirling smoke to the top of a Yumi tree.

'Boris,' said Matthew John. 'Was that you I heard wailing? What's up?'

'Goats are eating my leaves,' said Boris in his slow, weighty voice. 'I am a tree. I need my leaves to keep me warm. I need my leaves to breathe.' He scratched his long wooden nose with a slender, woody shoot.

'I don't see any goats eating your leaves,' said Matthew John, fanning the smoke with his hand and peering about him. It was hard to see anything, to tell the truth.

A goat named Cheeky landed in front of Prang and bared its teeth. 'Can't catch me! Waa!' said Cheeky, and leapt out of sight.

'I must remain calm,' said Prang to himself. 'I must breathe deeply.'

Three more goats landed in front of Prang and showed their teeth.

'Can't catch me! Waa!' shouted the first goat.

'Can't catch me! Waa!' shouted the second goat.

'Can't catch me! Waa!' shouted the third goat.

All three goats leapt into the smoke and vanished.

Prang shivered his wings. This was not his sort of mission. He heard loud munching sounds.

'What you hear,' said Boris, gravely, 'is the sound of my leaves being eaten. Is there nothing you can do, Matthew John?'

'I'll ask Mr. Seeds,' said Matthew John. 'He knows just about everything. He'll know what to do about the goats.'

Mr. Seeds was in his kitchen. He took a Mud Slide Ice Cream Cake out of his fridge and ladled hot chocolate sauce over it.

'Not bad,' said Prang. 'You bite through the hot chocolate sauce into the cold vanilla ice cream. Mm! Can I have another piece?'

Mr. Seeds gave Prang a second piece of cake. 'They are mountain goats, and very good at leaping,' he said. 'They fled from the mountain when the eruption began. They are eating the leaves of the Yumi trees because they are hungry.'

'Perhaps if I talked to the goats?' suggested Matthew John.

Mr. Seeds shook his head. 'Goats prefer eating to talking,' he said.

'Is there no way to drive the goats from the forest?' asked Matthew John.

'I wonder,' said Mr. Seeds. He wheeled his chair to the window and peered out at the rumbling mountain. 'At the end of Big Cat Canyon,' he said, 'you will find an entrance to the Lava Tubes.'

'The Lava Tubes?' said Matthew John, frowning. 'I don't think I've heard of those.'

'The Lava Tubes of Boom,' said Mr. Seeds, 'are a maze of underground passages. A tigress has her den somewhere in the Lava Tubes. Her name is Baagh. Find her, ask her politely, and she might scare the goats out of the forest.'

'I'll find her,' said Matthew John.

'Be careful,' said Mr. Seeds. 'She is a cunning tigress. Whatever you do, don't pull her tail. Where is your bat Bulmer today?'

'Bulmer was last seen giving a flying lesson to the group captain's brother, Gabriel Logan,' said Matthew John. 'He and the boy seem to have got themselves lost.'

'Lost, you say?' said Mr. Seeds.

'Prang and I are searching for them now. If I were group captain, I'd be organizing a proper search, but I'm only a wing commander, and my group captain is away serving on the starship Artibeus. Apparently that is what happens when you become a group captain. You leave the planet for a while and spend time in space.' Matthew John sighed. 'Prang,' he said. 'Finish up that third slice of Mud Slide Ice Cream Cake, and help me with the dishes. We're off to see a tigress.'

'A tigreth?' said Prang, with his mouth full.

'Goodbye, Mr. Seeds,' said Matthew John.

'Good luck, Matthew John,' said Mr. Seeds.

Matthew John mounted Prang, and they took to the air. Matthew John called his friends on his bat rider phone.

Within minutes, Matthew John and his companions were flying into Big Cat Canyon.

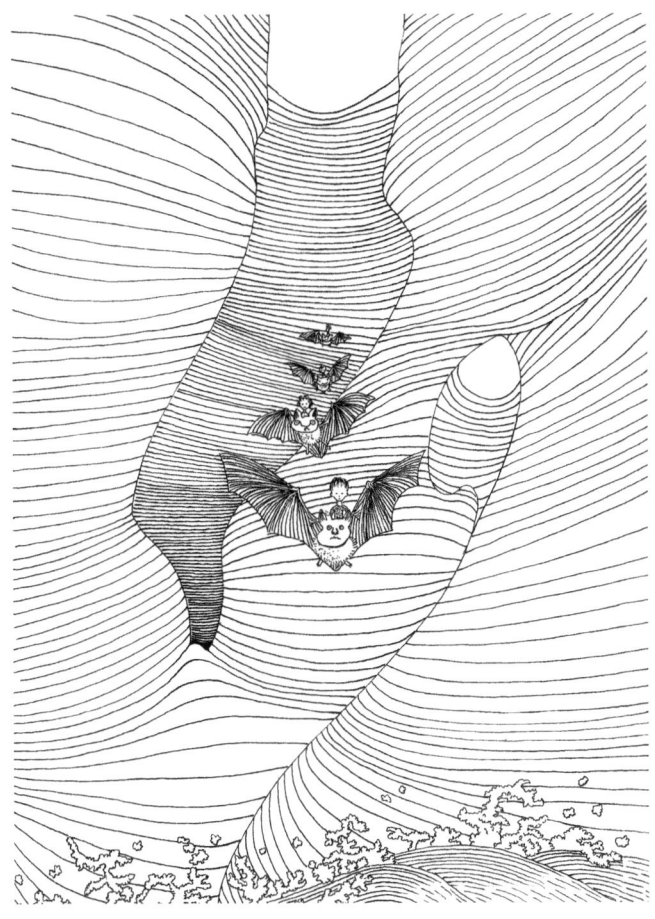

They flew in single file. Behind Matthew John, riding on Prang, Emily Charlotte rode her bat Vesper. Behind her, Joshua Ryan rode his bat Smoky, while Annabelle Sue rode in the rear on her bat Hula.

The canyon was loud with the sound of Big Cat River. Rocky walls tore by to their right and to their left. Below them white water heaved and thundered.

Spray from the river wet Matthew John's face. 'Wow!' he said. 'I wish Bulmer could see this.' He missed Bulmer more than he could say.

They came to a sudden turn and swooped to follow the canyon around the sharp corner. The canyon doubled back and they swooped the other way.

'All this swooping is making me dizzy,' said Prang.

When they arrived at the head of the canyon, the four bat riders landed in a dim grotto bright with the flowers of golden currant, wild cucumber and purple nightshade.

Matthew John leapt off Prang's back. He snatched a pair of flying goggles from the floor of the grotto. 'Bulmer borrowed these goggles from me this morning. He must have dropped them here. He can't be far away.'

Holding the goggles in one hand, Matthew John parted the flowering vines with his other hand.

'I think I've found the Lava Tubes of Boom,' he said.

'Let's have a look,' said Joshua Ryan.

Matthew John's friends pressed forward eagerly.

A lava tube stretched away into the distance. The walls of the tube were curvy and smooth, with thick yellow and orange veins that glowed in the dark. The tube had a sandy floor.

'I see four-toed paw prints in the sand,' said Matthew John.

They heard the thunder of approaching hooves. A herd of goats raced towards them down the lava tube, bleating with fear.

'Waa! Waa! Waa!' cried the goats, wide-eyed.

The goats ran past without stopping.

'Something must have scared those goats,' said Prang.

They watched the goats tear around a corner and vanish from sight.

'This is going be dangerous,' said Vesper. 'Don't say I didn't warn you.'

'Let's have a parade,' said Prang, hopefully. 'I am sure it must be time for a parade.'

'No parades until we find my bat Bulmer,' said Matthew John, and led the way into the lava tube, the flying goggles dangling from his hand.

The lava tube was too narrow for flying, so they went on foot, heading in the direction the goats had come from. The bats found the going difficult because their feet were joined to their wings, and they kept slipping and sliding in the sand.

In the lava tube ahead, a creature growled.

Wrrrrrr!

'Sounds like a tiger,' said Matthew John.

WRRRRRRR!

Kiti crouched down low, her tail quivering. She was trying out her tunnel vision. Tunnel vision is exciting. You look at your prey so hard you can't see anything else. It is a thrill. You wait and wait for your prey to run away. Then, when it runs away, you chase after it. The cardboard box Kiti was playing with wasn't very good at being the prey. It did not run away. It just sat there and did nothing.

'Bor-ing!'

Kiti stretched herself and yawned, to make her prey think she was too sleepy to attack.

'WRRRRRRR!' said Kiti, and leapt.

She caught the box off guard. She gave the box a fierce blow with her paw.

The box skittered sideways across the sandy bottom of the lava tube. That was better. Now Kiti could see inside the box. The box was empty. She ran at the box and leapt inside.

The box smelled of bat riders.

'Purp!' said Kiti, enjoying herself.

She scrabbled at the cardboard. Suddenly the box flipped over, and her whole world went dark.

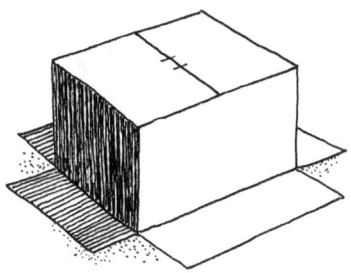

Instantly, she switched to night vision. Night vision was even more exciting than tunnel vision. With night vision, Kiti could see things others could not see.

'PURP! PURP!' said Kiti. Her voice sounded hollow inside the upside-down box, deeper and more grown-up.

'WRRRRRRR!' she said again, trying out her new, echoing voice. 'I AM YOUR WORST NIGHTMARE!' That was spine-chilling. That would really make her prey tremble. It was fun being a tigress, even if you were a very small tigress trapped inside a cardboard box. Just wait until her mother came back! She'd show her! Her mother would come back to the den and think: 'Oh! Where is my cub? And what is this cardboard box doing here?' and all the time Kiti would be hiding inside the box, and being very quiet and saying nothing, and then suddenly Kiti would surprise her mother. 'WRRRRRRR!' she would say. Perhaps that was her mother coming now? Kiti strained to hear.

Matthew John, Prang, his friends and their bats lay on their stomachs behind a rock parapet, peering at some creature they could barely see. The creature was moving about on the other side of a heaving river of red-hot bubbling rock. The lava tube was a little taller and wider here, and there was just enough room to fly.

'I AM YOUR WORST NIGHTMARE!' said a muffled voice.

'I told you we'd meet something awful,' said Emily Charlotte's bat Vesper.

'We come in peace!' said Matthew John loudly. 'We have a message for Baagh.'

'I AM DEATH ON FOUR LEGS!' was the reply.

Matthew John whispered to his companions. 'I think the voice is coming from that cave on the far side of the river of flowing lava.' He pulled his goggles down over his eyes. 'I can see tiger paw prints leading in and out of the den, but I can't see the tiger. Wait! I see something now. It looks like... a cardboard box.'

'A cardboard box?' said Annabelle Sue, drumming her fingers on her thighs. 'Who cares about a cardboard box?'

'The cardboard box is walking,' said Matthew John.

'Don't be silly,' said Annabelle Sue. 'Cardboard boxes don't walk.'

'This one does,' said Matthew John. 'Now the box is running. It has four legs. It's charging across the den. It going to hit the wall...'

'I AM YOUR... OW!' said the voice from the box.

'The box has hit the wall,' said Matthew John, 'and now the box is turning around. It is charging off in the opposite direction. It's going to hit the other wall.'

'I AM DEATH ON... OOF!' said the voice from the box.

'It has hit the other wall,' said Matthew John. He raised his voice. 'Stay where you are, Death-on-Four-Legs! We'll come and help you.'

The box went crazy. It spun around and charged off again.

'Look out!' shouted Matthew John. 'You're heading for the mouth of your den.'

'WRRRRRRR!' said the box.

'Stop!' shouted Matthew John. 'You'll fall off the cliff!'

'I AM... AAAAAH!'

'The box has fallen off the cliff,' said Matthew John.

'The box has landed on a ledge,' said Emily Charlotte.

'I don't need my goggles any more,' said Matthew John, removing them from his eyes. 'I can see the box by the glow of the red-hot lava river. The box has tipped over on its side. A creature has fallen out of the box.'

'It's a tiger cub,' said Prang.

'Oh, she's so cute!' said Emily Charlotte. 'Just look at her! A pretty little tiger club with yellow and black stripes! I can see her pink tongue. I love her to pieces.' She cupped her hands around her mouth. 'What's your name, little cub?'

The tiger cub looked at her scornfully. 'You wait until I get my teeth. I won't be your little tiger cub then. I'll be Kiti the Terrible. I'll have you for breakfast.'

'Way to go, Kiti,' said Annabelle Sue. 'Tell it like it is. Now hurry back into your den. I can see a fresh wave of lava coming. You're not safe on that ledge.'

'WRRRRRRR!' Kiti took an angry swipe at the cardboard box.

The box tumbled into the river of lava.

'I don't think Kiti understands that she's in danger,' said Annabelle Sue's bat Hula. 'She's going to be swept away by the lava.'

Emily Charlotte gasped. 'She's jumped into the box. She's floating down the lava river. The box is starting to burn. What can we can do?'

'We can rescue her,' said Matthew John, leaping on Prang's back. 'Prang, fly that tiger cub to safety.'

'Me?' said Prang, startled. 'Me? Be a hero? Yes, sir.' He came to attention, clicked his heels together, saluted smartly, and launched himself into space.

The fresh wave of lava arrived as he took off. Prang was caught in an updraft and thrown against the wall of the lava tube. The other bat riders and their bats backed away from the searing heat.

Prang tumbled down among them, his wings singed and smarting. 'Ouch!' he said. 'I don't think I'm very good at being a hero.'

Matthew John fell off Prang's back. He bumped his knee. He rubbed the sore place as he scrambled to his feet. He looked about him in dismay.

There was no sign of Kiti.

Emily Charlotte covered her face with her hands. 'The poor little tiger cub,' she whispered. 'Gone. Just like that.'

'You did your best, Prang,' said Matthew John. 'How do you feel? Are you badly hurt?'

'I'm okay,' said Prang. 'As I hit the wall, I thought I saw another bat through the smoke, and I thought I heard the other bat say "Chocks away!" What does "Chocks away!" mean?'

'It means nothing,' said Annabelle Sue. 'There was no other bat.'

'Listen!' said Vesper. 'Somebody's coming. I bet we're in for a really nasty surprise.'

The tigress Baagh ran as fast as she could through the Lava Tubes of Boom. When hunting, she could run at 35 miles an hour, but in an emergency she could run faster, and this was an emergency. She sensed that her cub was in danger. She tore through the tunnel at 50 miles an hour, her powerful legs moving with such speed and grace she seemed to float from pace to pace. She had left her daughter Kiti alone in their den with a cardboard box to play with. The air in Baagh's throat tasted of smoke, and she could smell burning lava. Would she be in time to save her cub? She shouted her own name out loud to let Kiti know she was coming.

'Baagh!' hollered the tigress. 'Baagh!'

Her cries shook the mountain.

Away in the forest, the goats stopped munching on the leaves of the Yumi trees and stared at one another.

In the caves where the bat riders lived, the boys and girls of Numbers Four and Five squadrons, asleep in their hammocks, woke with a start and wondered where their wing commander was, and what kind of strange beast was crying out from the mountain's heart.

Baagh charged on down the tunnel. The striped walls of the lava tube glowed brighter and brighter. Soon the heat became terrific. She dug her claws into the sand and skidded to a stop. She peered through a hole in the floor.

'Kiti?' she said. Looking down into her den, Baagh saw only bubbling hot lava. She stood very still, her mind racing. The lava had melted the rocks. Her daughter was no more. She had come too late to save her.

'Baaaaaaaagh!' she wailed.

'Don't give up hope,' said a voice. 'Your Kiti may yet be alive.'

Baagh swung around and saw two boys, two girls and four bats. She narrowed her yellow eyes, lowered her belly to the ground, and twitched her tail.

'Who are you?' she asked.

'We are bat riders,' said the smaller of the boys.

With a swipe of her paw, Baagh knocked the boy off the ledge and onto the floor. She put a paw on his chest. The boy lay on his back, looking up at her. 'Baagh?' he croaked, trying to get his breath back.

Baagh opened her mouth wide to show how many teeth she had and how sharp they were, and shoved her face close to the boy's. The boy smelled of Mud Slide Ice Cream Cake.

'Where is Kiti?' Baagh growled. 'Where is my daughter?'

'With Bulmer,' croaked Matthew John. 'I think.'

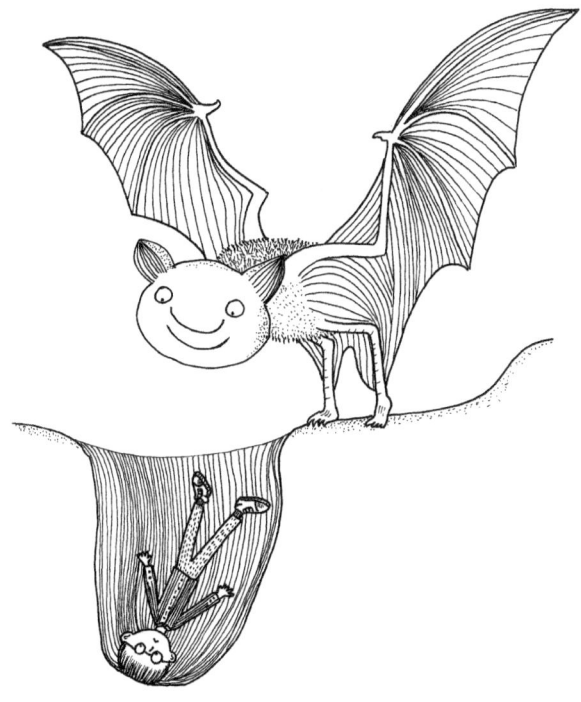

Bulmer and the group captain's brother, Gabriel Logan, had hit the ground hard.

'I shouldn't have tried a hammerhead right after a humpty-bump,' said Bulmer. 'Are you okay?'

'No, I'm not okay. I'm upside down in some kind of dark hole, and I can't see,' said Gabriel Logan, the group captain's brother.

'Lucky you can't see what I can see,' said Bulmer, staring at a glowing river of lava. He had never before seen red-hot rock on the move.

'Get me out of this, you stupid bat. Get me out of this right now,' said Gabriel Logan. 'You're supposed to be teaching me to fly. You don't even know how to land. When I'm a bat rider, I'll have myself a proper bat.'

A terrible cry echoed through the passages of the mountain. 'Baaaaaaaagh!'

'What's that?' said Gabriel Logan, climbing out of the hole in a hurry.

'I dunno,' said Bulmer. 'Sounds like a tiger.'

'A tiger?' said Gabriel Logan, his voice dropping to a whisper.

'A big cat with stripes,' said Bulmer.

'I know what a tiger is,' said Gabriel Logan between his clenched teeth. He was astonished to find himself seated at the edge of a channel filled with bubbling molten rock. The lava was flowing faster than he could run. He wiped sweat from his forehead. The air shimmered. He felt like a Yumi pie being baked in an oven.

'We're inside a lava thingy,' said Bulmer.

'What's that object floating in the lava?' asked Gabriel Logan.

'It looks like an old cardboard box,' said Bulmer. 'It's beginning to smoke around the edges. Uh. Lava is hot, you see. Lava sets things on fire.'

'I know that lava is hot,' said Gabriel Logan. 'You don't have to explain.'

A pair of paws appeared on the edge of the box and a small head appeared between them. 'I AM YOUR WORST NIGHTMARE,' said the small head.

'You don't look like my worst nightmare,' said Gabriel Logan, frowning. 'You look like a tiger cub.'

'What's your name?' asked Bulmer.

'I'm Kiti,' said the tiger cub.

'Have no fear, Kiti,' said Bulmer. 'Bulmer is here. Hop on my back, Gabriel Logan, and we'll save this tiger cub.'

With Gabriel Logan clinging to his back, Bulmer flew out over the river of lava and crashed into the floating cardboard box. He fell on his face.

'Lucky I fell inside the box,' he said, rubbing his nose.

Red-hot lava spattered the ceiling. The box rocked, threatening to tip bat, boy, and cub into the heaving molten rock.

'Grab that cub, Gabriel Logan,' said Bulmer. 'Quick!'

Gabriel Logan grasped Kiti firmly by the loose skin at the back of her neck, and hauled the young tigress up in front of him.

'Go, Bulmer!' he said.

'Chocks away!' said Bulmer, and flung himself up into the air.

The force of Bulmer's takeoff flipped the cardboard box over onto its side.

The box burst into flames.

'Just in time,' said Gabriel Logan, straightening his spectacles and looking back over his shoulder at the burning box.

'I can't wait to tell Matthew John,' said Bulmer. He missed Matthew John. He had no idea where Matthew John was or what he was doing.

Matthew John was in trouble. His breath had been knocked out of his lungs by a tigress. The tigress's face was inches from his. Her breath smelled of onions. He could see down her throat. He felt the weight of her huge paw pressing down on his chest. Flaming lava danced in her eyes.

138

'Where's… my… daughter?' said Baagh.

'Lemmebreepleeth,' said Matthew John, meaning that he wanted the tigress to let him breathe, please.

Baagh brought her face closer to his. 'Where… is… Kiti?' she growled.

'Wannanobetherlemego,' said Matthew John, meaning that if the tigress wanted to know, then she had better let him go.

Baagh pressed harder on Matthew John's chest. 'Tell me!' she said.

'Eye-fee wooey,' said Matthew John, meaning that he felt woozy.

'He can't breathe, you silly tigress,' said Annabelle Sue, pushing angrily at Baagh's nose. 'You're pressing too hard. Don't you have a brain? Can't you see he's choking?'

Baagh took some of the weight off Matthew John's chest. 'Where's… my… daughter?' she said again.

Matthew John felt air rush back to fill his lungs. 'We can help you find your daughter,' he said, 'if you help us first.'

'Help you?' said Baagh. 'How?'

'Our bats walk too slowly to escape the lava. Will you please carry us to safety? If you do, we'll do our best to find Kiti,' he said.

'What makes you think my daughter is still alive?' said Baagh, narrowing her eyes.

'We saw her leave the den before the lava arrived,' said Matthew John, 'and Prang heard another bat say "Chocks away!" We could not see clearly because of the smoke, but I think that bat may have been Bulmer.'

'Climb onto my back,' said the tigress.

All four riders and their bats climbed onto Baagh's back.

'This can't be happening,' said Prang, faintly. 'I can't be riding on the back of a tiger.'

'I'm not a tiger,' said Baagh, 'I'm a tigress.'

'Hang on tight, Prang,' said Matthew John, 'and keep your head down.'

Baagh began to run down the lava tube, following the course of the lava river.

Riding on Baagh's back was like riding a rollercoaster. Matthew John could feel the big cat's muscles rippling beneath him. The yellow and orange veins of the lava tube flicked past at astonishing speed.

'Whee!' said Smoky.

'We're riding on the tigress express!' said Joshua Ryan.

'I hope the tigress express knows where she's going,' said Hula.

Baagh charged down a lava tube, her breath coming in shuddering gasps. The lava tube was blocked by bubbling lava. She turned around and ran down another lava tube instead.

'She hasn't a clue,' said Vesper. 'We shall all be burned to cinders. I told you something awful would happen. Now it's happening.'

Karambamba, muttered Mount Boom. Babarumba!

Lava exploded from the tunnel wall, filling the air with cinders. Behind them, the ceiling of the lava tube melted and collapsed. Fresh lava rushed in.

'Do you know the way out?' shouted Matthew John in the tigress's ear.

'No,' answered Baagh. 'The lava tubes are changing. There may not be a way out.' She made a right turn and bolted down a narrow fissure hissing with escaping gas.

The fissure split into three.

'Which way?' asked Baagh.

Matthew John caught a glimpse of flowering vines.

'The left-hand lava tube,' he shouted.

Baagh streaked down the left-hand lava tube, burst through a hanging curtain of golden currant, wild cucumber and purple nightshade, and came to a halt in the open air.

'I can see the sky!' said Emily Charlotte.

'We have escaped from the Lava Tubes!' said

Joshua Ryan.

'We're still in trouble,' said Matthew John, looking around him. He could see streams of lava coursing down the mountainside both to left and to right. 'Mount your bats, everyone!'

Matthew John and his friends took off from Baagh's back. They flew high into the air. Soon they could see the entire mountain spread out below them, obscured here and there by drifting clouds of smoke.

'Head for the forest!' shouted Matthew John, pointing with his arm to show Baagh which way to run.

The tigress ran like the wind down the mountain, heading for the Yumi trees.

'Baagh!' she cried as she ran, hoping to hear her cub answer her.

She heard nothing.

'Baagh!' she shouted again.

She tore into the forest.

'A tiger has come to eat us!' cried Cheeky Goat. 'Run for your lives, goats!'

'Waa!' shouted the goats.

All of the goats leapt from the Yumi trees and charged out of the forest. The goats ran past Mr. Seeds's house. They stampeded into the Sleepy Field. 'Hide among these bushes, goats! We'll be safe here,' said Cheeky Goat, and he sank to his knees. 'Oo! I feel sleepy,' he said. He and all his fellow goats fell asleep kneeling. That is how goats sleep.

Baagh dug her claws into the ground and ploughed to a halt on the lawn in Mr. Seeds's garden. She stood there, panting. She had run for miles. She was far enough from the mountain to be safe from the lava. A lump came into her throat. The bats and their riders had deserted her. She would never see her daughter again. 'Oh, Kiti,' she said. She lay down and rested her head on her front paws. Her eyes filled with tears.

Mount Boom stopped rumbling. The eruption came to an end.

Matthew John and his friends flew back and forth over the cooling mountainside searching for the missing bat, rider and cub. The boys and girls of both squadrons joined them in the search.

As they flew to and fro, the bat riders saw the lava turn grey. One by one, the rivers of lava slowed to a halt. The lava turned to stone. In the forest, a bird began to sing.

'It's over,' said Prang. 'Can we go home now?'

Matthew John's heart was heavy. He had lost his bat and best friend. He had failed to find Baagh's daughter, and failed to rescue his group captain's brother. His mission was a failure. He sighed and reached for his bat rider phone. 'I'm ending the search for today,' he said. 'Back to your caves, bat riders. Thank you all for your help.' He put away his phone. 'We had better go and tell Mr. Seeds the bad news,' he said.

Mr. Seeds made them scrambled eggs on toast and added a sprig of parsley from his garden to each dish. Matthew John helped to carry the food from the kitchen outside onto the lawn, where Baagh lay with her head on her paws. The tigress was too big to invite inside the house, and too miserable to eat.

Mr. Seeds wheeled his chair outside. 'You must be exhausted after your adventure,' he said. 'Don't feel too badly. Not all missions succeed.'

'I miss Bulmer so,' said Matthew John. 'I used to laugh at him for landing on his nose. He was the best of bats.'

'I miss Gabriel Logan,' said the group captain, who had just returned from a tour of duty on the starship Artibeus. He was dismayed to hear that his brother was missing. The group captain looked up at the sky and swallowed. The searchers had gone home. The sky was empty. He might never see his brother again.

'I miss my cub Kiti,' said Baagh, raising her head and looking at Matthew John. 'She loved playing with her cardboard box. She used to jump on top of her box and growl. Life will not be the same without her.'

'I'm so sorry,' said Matthew John, rubbing the sore place on his knee.

The bat riders, their bats, Mr. Seeds, the group captain and Baagh all looked at one another as people do after a disaster, stunned by the loss of those they love.

'Watch out!' said a voice from above. 'I'm no good at landing.'

Matthew John looked up in astonishment. 'Bulmer?' he said 'Is that you?'

Skimming low over the roof of the house came a battered bat, his wings singed by lava and his pink ears torn. The bat was so tired he could scarcely beat his wings. It was Bulmer. On Bulmer's back crouched a boy and a tiger cub. Both were hanging on for dear life.

'Home sweet home,' said Bulmer, and skidded across the grass, flailing his wings desperately.

'Can't seem to stop!' he said, as he skidded past Mr. Seeds. 'No brakes!' he said as he slid past the group captain. 'Heading for the fountain!' he said as he slid past Baagh.

At the last moment, to save himself from ending up in the fountain, Bulmer grabbed the tail of the tigress with his teeth.

'BAAGH!' said Baagh, and sprang high into the air. She was outraged. Nobody but Kiti had ever dared to bite her tail. She would teach this miserable bat a lesson he would never forget. She raised her paw.

'Way to go, Mummy!' said a small voice. 'Give it to the bat!'

Baagh's jaw dropped. 'Kiti?' she said, and forgot all about the bat, she was so delighted to see her cub again. She wrapped her arms around her daughter. She smothered her with kisses. 'Snuggle-ums!' she cried. 'My cookie-wooky-baby!'

Kiti squirmed. 'I wish you wouldn't, Mummy,' the cub hissed. 'It's embarrassing. We're supposed to be tigers.'

'Tigresses, dear,' said Baagh, holding her cub at arm's length and looking her over carefully to make sure she had come to no harm. 'How did you escape from the lava?'

'I hit the box,' said Kiti, 'and the box went in the lava and then I jumped in the box and then the boy and the bat jumped in too, and then the box fell over but the bat took off, and then I rode on the bat's back, and flew through a cloud and hit the lawn.'

'It sounds as if you had a good time,' said Baagh. 'We must thank these bat riders and their bats.'

'Can we eat them now?' said Kiti.

'Not today,' said Baagh.

'Your den has been destroyed, Baagh,' said Mr. Seeds. 'The bats might let you share their cave if you promise not to eat them.'

146

Bulmer opened his mouth, letting go of the tail of the tigress. 'I think I burnt my wings,' he said.

Matthew John ran for a fresh jar of Make-You-Better butter from Mr. Seeds's store, and slathered the healing ointment on Bulmer's wings. 'Poor Bulmer,' he said. 'This should make you feel better.'

'It does feel cool and nice,' said Bulmer. 'Thanks, Matthew John.' He lowered his voice. 'I'm afraid I did a humpty-dump before a hammerhead. Gabriel Logan was angry with me.'

'I shouldn't worry, Bulmer. Gabriel Logan has other things on his mind right now,' said Matthew John. 'His big brother has just come back from space.'

'Welcome home, brother,' said Gabriel Logan, shaking the hand of the group captain. 'How was it serving on the Artibeus?'

'She's a fine ship,' the group captain replied. 'We had a little brush with the Mormoops but we came through all right. What have you been up to?'

'I have been learning to fly,' said Gabriel Logan. 'I'm going to be a bat rider.'

'Good for you,' said the group captain. 'My flying days are over. You can have my bat, if you like.'

'Can I really? What's your bat called? Does your bat know how to land?'

'Her name is Pinky. She lands on her head,' said the group captain, and then put his fingers in his mouth and whistled. A black velvet bat with pink eyes flashed down from the sky and landed on her head.

'Pinky, this is Gabriel Logan. He's looking for a bat to ride.'

'Blimey!' said Pinky. 'He's a midget.'

Matthew John, overhearing the remark, said 'Think tall and you won't feel small.' That had been the advice his father had given him on his own first day as a bat rider.

Gabriel Logan hopped on Pinky's back. 'Let's go, Pinky!' he said.

'Would you care to loop the loop?' said Pinky, as the pair took off.

The group captain watched them fly away. 'You're the new group captain now, Matthew John,' he said, and reached into his pocket. 'Stand still for a moment while I pin this medal on your chest.'

'A medal?' said Matthew John, surprised. He fingered the gold disk with awe. He had never had a medal before. 'What's it for?'

'It's a medal for being brave. Mr. Seeds tells me you led your bat riders into the Lava Tubes of Boom and discovered the den of Baagh.'

'I don't deserve a medal,' said Matthew John. 'We were nearly roasted alive, and anyway it was Bulmer who saved Gabriel Logan and Kiti. He's the one who should have the medal, not me.'

'Don't pin that medal on me,' said Bulmer. 'I'm sore enough already. Look! Here come your parents.'

Mummy and Daddy hurried over to hug Matthew John and congratulate him on his medal and on his promotion.

'Well done, Matthew John,' said Daddy. 'Your starship awaits you.'

ARTI BEUS

CHAPTER VI

Putting the Bats to Bed

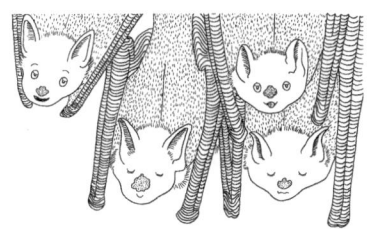

'**P**ut the bats to bed,' says Matthew John, yawning. 'I'll be there soon.'

I gather the drowsy bats up in my arms and carry them all inside their cave. One by one, I hang the bats upside down from the ceiling.

'Don't forget to lock your feet,' I remind them.

'Did Matthew John really go on a starship?' asks Hula, sleepily.

'I'm not sure,' I say. 'You can ask him when you wake up.'

'I expect he got lost in space,' says Vesper.

'I wouldn't be surprised,' I say.

'Matthew John was afraid of the dark,' says Pinky, 'but he was brave and went into the cave anyway.'

'And that's how he met Bulmer,' says Suki.

'Can we have another story?' asks Misty.

'Not now,' I say. 'Wrap yourself up in your wings and close your eyes.'

ABOUT THE AUTHOR

Anthony Barton lives in Canada by the sea. As he writes about Matthew John and Bulmer, mountains of ice float past his window. After sunset little brown bats appear, darting through the air and making peeping sounds. For the first few days, the young bat clings to its mother. She has only one baby, but her child grows up quickly, and may live for more than twenty years. Anthony Barton has a website where you may find out more about bats, and read more stories about Matthew John and Bulmer. The website is anthonybarton.com

FREE BAT RIDER SERIAL

An Audio Serial for Boys and Girls
by the Same Author
Anthony Barton

Bat Rider and the Cave of Oomba

Bat Rider and the Cave of Oomba is an eight-part serial.
Narration is by the author, with music, bat squeaks and production by
Siri Arnet. All eight episodes are free and may be heard at
Podiobooks.com

COMING SOON

A New Book for Boys and Girls
by the Same Author
Anthony Barton

The Yumi Trees

The Yumi Trees is the sequel
to *Bat Rider*. The mile-high Yumi trees
are in danger and Matthew John and his friends
must brave a tidal wave and make friends with the
oldest tree in the forest in their bid to save them.

One reviewer writes:

'A children's world is inevitably one built
around colossal changes and an unavoidable
"metamorphosis" as they grow up. Suddenly
they can do things themselves and parents
can be a bit embarrassing but deeply loved!
For your children, assuming they have read
all of the Matthew John adventures and
have drawn close to all the Bat Riders,
The Yumi Trees provides a powerful
new step forward in their lives.'

The Yumi Trees will be available as a printed book
with illustrations by the author
from Amazon.com

NOW AVAILABLE

E-Books for Boys and Girls

The Bat Rider Adventures